# The Royal Road

## Robin Saxon

Dreamspinner Press

Published by
Dreamspinner Press
5032 Capital Circle SW
Ste 2, PMB# 279
Tallahassee, FL 32305-7886
USA
http://www.dreamspinnerpress.com/

The Royal Road

Cover Art by Shobana Appavu
bob@bob-artist.com

ISBN: 978-1-62380-305-6
Digital ISBN: 978-1-62380-306-3

Printed in the United States of America
First Edition
January 2013

To Alex.
"For this was on seynt Volantynys day
Whan euery bryd comyth there to chese his make."

The interpretation of dreams is the royal road to a knowledge of the unconscious activities of the mind.

—Sigmund Freud
*The Interpretation of Dreams*

# Chapter One

—▪—▪——▪——▪——▪——▪——▪——▪———▪——▪———▪—

STEPHEN grasped William's hip tightly, using his free hand to rip William's shirt open. The delicate pearl buttons scattered to the corners of Stephen's lush but comfortable living room.

"Oh, Stephen!" William gasped, throwing his head back, his blond hair tumbling over his shoulders like a chaotic waterfall. "You are so strong! Use your manly strength on me, you fine-looking masculine specimen!"

Thoughtfully twiddling his moustache between his fingers, Stephen gazed at William's exposed chest, which was heaving like the sea crashing against a rocky shore, arching toward Stephen like a plant desperately seeking the sun for photosynthesis. Stephen smiled wickedly. "My William, before this night is over, you shall know I have strength like no other. My strength is mightier than ten men combined. Perhaps even ten and a half."

William gasped again, nervously biting a plush, bee-stung lower lip. "Yes, oh yes, Stephen, use your supple but well-defined muscles on me!"

With an incredible tearing sound, Stephen threw his own shirt off. His chest gleamed bronze in the low light. Stephen was more muscular than the Roman gladiators of old, more enchanting than Apollo himself, more handsome than the finest of models, more ripped than professional wrestlers without the steroids. William was simply overcome by the sheer majesty standing before him. His knees felt weak; his skin burned hotter than the sun.

"I can't tell you how much I love you," William cried. "I know we only met ten minutes ago after I accidentally ran over your dog, but you're it. You're my soul mate. My entire life is now going to revolve around you in a totally noncreepy, definitely not brainwashed way!"

Stephen flexed. William nearly fainted. "Of course you love me," Stephen replied. "I have no personality and don't care about your feelings. I am the catch of the century."

—+——+———+——+——+——+——+——+———+——+———+——

WESTON awoke with an ungainly snort, jerking his head up off his desk. The first thing to catch his bleary gaze was a streak of drool left on the polished wood, which he clumsily wiped at with his sleeve.

The clock on the wall informed him it was six in the morning.

He'd fallen asleep with his head on his desk, his left hand curled possessively around the handle of a long-cold mug of coffee. His laptop was open in front of him—a single document displaying a short snippet of a story. Three hundred words.

And every single one of those words was utter shit.

Weston groaned, squeezing his eyes shut as he rubbed his forehead. He had vague memories of a three-in-the-morning caffeine bender spent hunched over and staring at his laptop and hoping that by hitting the keys harder, he'd somehow write better. He'd wanted to write a romance.

Instead, there was this—this regurgitation of every bad stereotype in written romance, with baffling metaphors thrown in for good measure.

Weston very carefully selected all of it and deleted it. It made him feel a lot better.

His morning routine passed in a blur of coffee and too many differently colored shirts. Every morning was the same—Weston couldn't decide if he should go with the white shirt and the gray suit or the black shirt with the darker gray suit. Like every morning, a glance at the clock told him he was five minutes late, and he wished he had the mental discipline to do something like spend a few minutes in the evening to plan for the next day's clothing. It would certainly make his mornings a lot easier.

The radio blared too loud when he got into his car, and some advertisement with the sound of screeching tires made him curse and slap the Off button. It should, he thought, be illegal to have noises in radio advertisements that made him wonder if another car was going to crash into him.

When he finally pulled into the parking lot, Weston felt somewhat awake, aided by the travel mug of coffee. He raked his hands through his hair, studying the sliver of reflection he caught in the rear view mirror. A turn of his head revealed a spot that he'd somehow missed during shaving, a patch of stubble interrupting otherwise smooth skin low on his jaw.

Well, there was nothing for it. He could hardly drive back home just to clean up his shaving job.

The building he'd parked outside was small and built with brick; a cheery sign over the door proclaimed it was Sanderson Designs. A smaller sign below it read *We Help Bring Your Mascots to Life!* Weston pushed open the door, intending to head straight to the office. The bell above the doorframe jingled a little merrily for Weston's liking.

"You're five minutes late."

The bland voice dragged Weston out of his morning-induced misery. He forced his eyes upward, meeting the gaze of the Leech. "Huh?"

"You're five minutes late," the Leech replied. "If you want to keep your job and ensure that Sanderson Designs is efficient, you can't be constantly late."

The Leech, contrary to his nickname, was a perfectly ordinary person. Weston would even admit that the Leech—otherwise known as Sidney Romero—was not hard on the eyes at all. With perfectly fitted dark suits that complemented his olive complexion and dark hair, Sidney was exactly the sort of man Weston would otherwise enjoy flirting with.

Unfortunately, Sidney Romero was a productivity consultant. Hired to loiter around businesses, productivity consultants looked at everything. Profit, employee wages, overtime, unnecessary jobs, overpaid cleaners—they thoroughly examined every single dirty little secret and assessed whether they were helping or hindering the business.

Needless to say, as small business workers who casually took days off and enjoyed very long lunch breaks, none of Sanderson's employees were entirely happy about the new man in the office.

"Sure. I'll work on that." Weston figured he sounded unconvincing enough, so he made his way toward his office, cringing internally at the prickly sensation of eyes watching his back. He knew he was being watched, and judged accordingly.

His office, a generously sized room toward the front of the building, was as chaotic as ever. Weston smiled as he entered, immediately feeling a sense of relief among the scattered papers pinned haphazardly to the walls, the mess of pencils over his desk. He all but threw himself into his chair and began sorting through the designs stacked in his inbox.

He only glanced up as Henry closed the office door behind himself. "Can you believe this shit?" Henry said, giving an incredulous glance behind him, as if he could see through the door. "The Leech is already going off at me about fucking fabric."

Weston grinned at him. Henry was a close friend, made so because Weston thoroughly enjoyed his bluntness. "Yeah, I got told off for being five minutes late," he replied. "As if Sanderson gives a shit."

"Fucking *fabric*," Henry repeated. "He keeps telling me that if I order fabric from Smith's, not Easy Fabrics, then we'll save money. I keep telling him that he can go shove his foot up his ass."

Alarmed, Weston frowned at Henry. "You don't actually say that to him, do you?"

"No, but I'm definitely thinking it." Henry had worked himself up into a proper old-fashioned fit of scowling now. "We have a good relationship with Easy Fabrics. They like Sanderson, they prioritize our orders, and now the Leech wants us to shift to Smith's just because it'd be cheaper. It's not like we don't make up the cost by charging more."

Weston buried a sigh in the hand he rubbed across his mouth. "Maybe he has a point there," he said reluctantly.

"No," Henry said. "He doesn't have a point. He has no point. Don't get brainwashed."

Henry was giving him such a severe, horrified look at the thought of betrayal that Weston had to laugh. "All right, all right," he relented. "You're right. We get as many buyers as we need, and Sanderson's always said he's happy with the level of profit we're making."

"Damn straight." Henry nodded, satisfied. "The Leech can go do his productivity shit at the big businesses that don't know their asses from their elbows."

Weston took a moment to contemplate this; he couldn't imagine a scenario in which someone would be so confused as to not know their ass from their elbow. "Unfortunately we're stuck with him for a few more weeks," he pointed out. At Henry's pained groan, Weston added, "But until then, we should find as many excuses as we can to throw office parties. Birthdays, anniversaries, foreign holidays, and personal tragedies. All of them should come with cake. Cake makes everything more bearable."

That was how Weston ended up sending an office-wide e-mail, first alerting everybody not to tell the Leech about the contents of the e-mail, then informing everybody that the next few weeks would have a heavy emphasis on personal achievements and the need to celebrate them.

He was alone in his office once more. Weston leaned back in his chair, staring at the scattered concept art he had pinned to his walls. His thoughts went back to what he'd written the previous night.

That had been some frankly terrible writing. Weston half laughed to himself at the memory of his attempt at being an author as he absently went through e-mails. In the back of his mind, there was a place littered with cobwebs and forgotten ideas; it was the place Weston stored all of his futile hopes, one of which was being a writer. He wanted to write the kinds of things that evoked emotion in others, painted beautiful imagery and grand ideas.

He didn't lack ideas. No, Weston had *plenty* of ideas. He spent half his day thinking about moss-covered castles and the golden dragons flying over them, of puddle-ridden back alleys where murderers skulked, of love so incredible it couldn't be hidden. He had ideas. He just couldn't write them. His every attempt at writing them came out riddled with clichés, a half-sarcastic criticism on the stereotypes of the genre he was trying to write in.

The gleaming golden dragons flying over crumbled castles were all well and good for a painting, but what of a novel? There, Weston would have to concentrate on the characters. The wealthy kings and the beggars, the bards playing on their old wooden instruments, and the plucky heroines who saved the day.

But there his ability ended. He just couldn't seem to write any of them.

And when he woke up in the mornings, he came here. Sanderson Designs. A small family business that designed mascot costumes for sports teams. He worked in an office in a job that had no imagination—sure, he designed things, but he designed the *same* things. Over and over. Cartoonish faces and fluffy bodies. He took his lunch breaks and ate while he stared out the window that looked out onto the highway. He clocked in, and he worked, and he left.

Weston wanted more.

# Chapter Two

—◆——◆——◆——◆——◆——◆——◆——◆——◆——◆——◆——◆——

"WINGBLADE! The danger draws near!"

WingBlade shielded his eyes from the glaring sun as he looked up into the periwinkle-blue sky. A shape, a dark shadow, was flying closer, mighty wings rending the air with every powerful beat.

"It's a dragon!" he bellowed, puffing out his strong chest with the force of his shout. "HardIron, muster the villagers and get them into hiding!"

His dwarven companion thumped his fist to his chest, his braided dark beard bobbing as he ran to do WingBlade's bidding. WingBlade spared a look at the small village—it was tiny, diminutive, and little. Made of thatched roofing and thin wood, it would not survive should the dragon decide to scorch it with its epic breath of flame.

Bravely, heroically, WingBlade drew his sword.

"You're the only one who can save us from this threat, Speaker WingBlade!" a villager shrieked as she ran past. "Only you are mighty enough to defeat this terrible evil!"

"I know," WingBlade said stoically. His was a heavy burden. It troubled him every day, tore at his heart and caught his breath, but he continued on. For that was the path of a DragonSpeaker.

The dragon landed with a deafening thump. Its red scales gleamed in the bright sunlight, and when it opened its jaws, its roar seemed to shake the very stones of the earth.

—+— —+— —+— —+— —+— —+— —+— —+— —+— —+— —+— —+—

"I WANT a puffer fish with a squirrel tail."

Mr. Kent was much like many businessmen Weston saw over the course of the day: just past middle aged, with a growing gut that protested the confines of his shirt, redness around his cheeks, and hair that was too harshly combed back. He stank as if he'd bathed in his cologne, which wafted aggressively at anybody who came within a ten-foot radius.

"A puffer fish with a squirrel tail," Weston repeated.

"Yes," Mr. Kent said. "And it has to be red."

Red like the dragon he'd written about last night. Weston idly wondered why a dragon would be red. If such a thing as dragons ever existed, it was more than likely they'd be green like their reptilian counterparts. It just made more sense from an evolutionary point of view. Things that brightly colored in nature tended to be so to advertise that they were poisonous, or were that way to attract mates.

Maybe that was why the dragon in his story had been red. Maybe they were a dying race, and they'd started taking on bright colors so they'd attract more mates.

The more pertinent question was: WingBlade? Seriously? That was the character's name? Had he really fallen into the stereotype of taking two nouns and mashing them together to create a fantasy name?

"It has to be a specific shade of red." Mr. Kent was still talking. Weston figured he should probably pay attention and not internally theorize about the evolutionary changes to a species regarding reproduction success. That probably wasn't appropriate to think about at work. "It's on the team's uniform. If the color is off by a shade, they won't match."

"Of course," Weston agreed. "That would be an absolute disaster."

"It would be." Mr. Kent nodded gravely. "I'm glad you understand. I'm glad I came to Sanderson Designs. It's this kind of quality attention-to-detail work I need, not the crap put out by those mass-producing companies who don't care about their customer."

Weston drew in a deep breath, trying to restrain himself from saying that he assumed the man came to Sanderson Designs because of his incredibly unusual request that no mass-production company would cater to, and not out of any urge to support a small business. Sadly, he figured saying that wouldn't be good for business.

"Well, I'll get a couple things drawn up and I'll get them to you by e-mail tomorrow. How does that work?" As Mr. Kent stood, Weston did too, and they shook hands across his desk. "I'd like to work with you closely to make sure you're happy with the design."

They made their farewells, and Weston continued to stand as he watched the portly man leave his office and walk down the hallway. He shook his head, bemused. A red puffer fish with a squirrel tail.

Well, at least it was different.

Half an hour later, the uniqueness of Mr. Kent's concept no longer entertained him. Weston growled under his breath and crumpled the paper he'd been sketching on. He threw it. It tumbled neatly into the trash can across his office.

"A perfect three-pointer," the Leech said dryly from the doorway.

Weston jerked, his knee coming up hard against the underside of the desk. "Ow, fuck! I mean—" Shit, what was a good tame curse word? "Damn?"

"My grandmother always said 'fudge'." The Leech—Sidney; Weston should really start remembering he had a name—wore an expression somewhere between forced casualness and irritation.

"I'll make sure to use that in the future," Weston replied as blandly as he could manage.

Sidney parted his lips as if to say something but closed them again, his response obviously dying before he said it. He then said, "I'm here to talk to you about your medium."

Maybe Weston hadn't had enough coffee that morning, because it took him a few seconds to puzzle that one out. No, Sidney was not talking about a person communicating with the dead. "Oh, my paper?" Weston took a look around his office. Was it too messy? "I guess I could tidy the stuff on the walls a bit."

Sidney made a little frown that looked like a grimace. "That's not what I meant. May I sit?"

That didn't bode well.

"Sure, pull up a chair," Weston offered, leaning back in his own seat.

"What I mean is that while your supplies, your paper and pencils, are cheap enough, I think there could be alternatives that would make things much more efficient," Sidney said. "I've spoken with Mr. Sanderson about this, and he agrees, hence why I'm bringing the idea to you."

That was even worse than what Weston had been expecting.

"But I like my paper," Weston replied, stunned. "What alternatives?"

Sidney put a slim magazine on his desk; the cover boasted its impressive range of art tablets. "I was thinking something like this. It depends on what model you want to get, but they're all well within the budget that Mr. Sanderson agreed to."

"But, my paper," Weston repeated dumbly. "I'm used to my notebooks and my pencils."

"This would also allow you to be much more organized." Sidney's expression softened. He looked as though he was trying to coax a terrified rabbit out of a comfortable warren. "Everybody is using them these days."

Sidney clearly did not get it.

"I *like my paper*," Weston stressed.

His emphasis didn't impress Sidney, though Weston was surprised to see an amused crinkle at the corner of Sidney's eyes.

"Did you have to get dragged, kicking and screaming, to upgrade to store-bought butter instead of churned?"

"Hey, I'm not *that* old," Weston protested. "I'm thirty-two."

"And you're as stubborn as an eighty-year-old who doesn't like those 'newfangled interwebs'."

Was Sidney laughing at him?

"I...." Weston chanced a look at the magazine on his desk. With such determined enthusiasm from Sidney, he had little choice but to give in. "Sure. I'll take a look." He fought the urge to clutch his notepad protectively to his chest.

"Good." Sidney almost smiled at him. "I know it's very different than what you're used to, but I think once you do get used to it, you'll never want to look back. I have a good friend who swears by these things."

Weston was just surprised that Sidney apparently had friends. Or, friend. Singular. Multiple friends had yet to be confirmed.

Sure, Sidney was a good-looking guy. He was a *great*-looking guy, actually, and Weston could picture him on a Friday evening, hanging out with friends at a local bar. Especially in the clothes he'd been wearing yesterday—business slacks and a deep-red shirt. The same red of the dragon in Weston's late-night caffeine-bender writing.

Weston was sure it was complete coincidence.

"Okay. Yeah, I'll give it a try." Weston found himself feeling a little encouraged by Sidney's slight smile. Did Sidney Romero actually have a soul? Weston had been half-convinced that he didn't, that he was part of some bland group of entities whose job it was to judge everything around them.

"Good. I'll leave you to your work then, Weston." Sidney gave him a polite nod and took his leave.

Weston glanced down at the magazine again and very tentatively flipped it open. He could admit that the products it advertised looked pretty cool. It meant he could draw and not have to worry about permanent mistakes, not to mention little eraser bits getting everywhere. It would even eliminate the step of having to scan his concept art to e-mail it to the client.

While studying the next page, he absently reached out to find his cup of coffee, only to discover with a sip that it had gone cold. Grimacing heavily, Weston put it aside and then reconsidered and picked it up to take with him on a walk to the office kitchen.

It wasn't anywhere near lunchtime, so the only other person in the kitchen was Aiko, impatiently tapping at the top of the coffee machine with bright-orange-painted fingernails. "Morning," she greeted vaguely, apparently more interested in watching the coffee slowly filter into the mug.

"Is that thing *still* going that slow?" Weston sighed, poured his cold coffee into the sink, and joined Aiko in staring despondently at the machine.

She answered him with a wordless affirmative noise.

Weston didn't subscribe to the philosophy of *coffee is my lifeblood* like some of his coworkers seemed to, but it did provide a nice perk-up in the morning. And at night, when he wrote. And at lunch. And there was a place on Fifth that did the best mochas. But he didn't *need* it. Of course not.

As he and Aiko stood together in impatient solidarity, Weston found his mind going back, yet again, to what he'd written last night. He vaguely recalled wanting to write high fantasy—he'd read piles of high fantasy when he was young, devouring them daily, spending his classes lost in worlds full of mystical forests and brave heroes. He'd wanted to write something of a love letter to them, an homage. Instead, his mind had obviously decided to take the most common stereotypes and write *that*.

Weston wanted to write something unique. Something new. He understood, rationally, that that probably wasn't possible. Every basic story had already been written; the only new thing an author could do was write a new spin on it, a new point of view, a new window dressing. But instead of coming up with something like that, his mind had gone to—

"'Sup, losers," Henry greeted tiredly, shuffling into the kitchen. "Fucking coffee machine at it again?"

Henry. Who was on the short side with a shock of dark hair and a closely cropped beard.

Henry, who suspiciously resembled Weston's mental image of the dwarf he'd written about last night, the one with the terrible name. HardIron.

"I wrote about you last night," Weston said cheerfully. "I was hopped up on caffeine and not making much sense, so I think I must have just written you in when I couldn't make up an original character. You were a dwarf. And you had a massive beard."

Henry treated him to a long disbelieving stare. "Weston," he said slowly, "I call you my friend, but you're actually fucking crazy, you know that?"

"You know who else is crazy?" Aiko made an irritated noise. "The Leech."

An equally irritated noise came from Henry, who promptly dropped the dwarf topic in favor of happily moving on to the Leech. "Yeah? What's he done now? Suggested to Sanderson that we all work an extra day?"

"He wants us to consolidate our computer software. Fuck that, I *like* my system. I've had it for years and it works for me." Aiko grabbed the cup of coffee that had just finished filling. "And can you imagine trying to shift Pat off her system?"

Weston couldn't help but laugh. "How long has she even been here? Seven years?"

"Eight," Henry corrected. He made a none-too-subtle step toward the coffee machine, scowling at Weston's smugly triumphant expression when Weston got there first. "And we all have our own way of doing things. We don't need to be homogenized or whatever to be efficient. So what if Pat prints off all her e-mails and handwrites her replies? She gets the job done!"

"Exactly!" Aiko made an aborted motion of her arm, as though she'd narrowly stopped herself from throwing it up in exasperation and remembered at the last second that she had a cup of hot coffee. "And now the Leech wants us to buy a whole bunch of new equipment so we can match. I swear to God, he's trying to put this company under."

"Actually...." Weston frowned. "I had a talk with him earlier. I almost hate to say this, but I guess he had a good idea."

While he was still digesting the baffling concept of making the switch from paper to tablet, he had to admit that he could see Sidney's point. It would certainly cut down on time spent scanning, processing, and e-mailing.

Now he just had to get over himself and break away from the opinion that drawing straight to the computer wasn't *cheating* because he could undo anything he wanted.

Henry looked at him as though he'd just grown a second head and it had started talking. "Dude. The Leech isn't a force for good."

"He's *evil*," Aiko said, squinting at him suspiciously. "He's a productivity consultant. All they ever do is make people's lives miserable."

"I'm just saying he isn't *that* bad," Weston protested.

"He's weird!" Aiko really did make an expansive gesture then—with the hand that wasn't too busy clutching her coffee. "He eats salads for lunch! With olives! And he's creepy—have you ever seen the way he watches people? And he never talks about anything that's not job related. I bet you he has no life. I bet he works and then goes home and just stares at the wall. For *fun*."

While Henry was laughing, Weston took his own finally prepared coffee. "I guess he is kind of quiet," he agreed tentatively.

His current theory was that Sidney was just an introvert stuck in an environment full of extroverts. Weston had been starting to think that maybe Sidney wasn't quiet in a creepy way, that maybe the rumors about him had been a little too harsh. In that last meeting, he'd seen Sidney smile. He hadn't seemed like the rumored secret axe murderer at all.

"He's *too* quiet." Aiko peered at Weston over the rim of her mug as she took a sip. "I don't like people who are too quiet. It makes me wonder what they're planning, or if they just hate me and they're too nice to tell me."

"Well, I don't think Sidney can be both evil *and* too nice," Weston pointed out.

Aiko stared back at him with all the expression of a rock.

"Maybe he's complicated?" Weston offered feebly.

Aiko blinked at him and shook her head. "Henry, can you check Weston for signs of a pod person? I have to get back to work." She left with a waft of perfume and the jingle of too many bracelets. Weston jerked away from Henry's hand, which Henry had put on his forehead.

"No fever, probably no pod people," Henry said gravely, a hint of a smirk at the edge of his expression. "But seriously, man, he's the Leech. Not *Sidney*. He's the enemy who wants us all to suffer."

Weston decided there was no use arguing. Henry was a good friend, and Weston liked Aiko—they were probably right. Maybe he was just trying to see good where there was none, because he didn't like the idea of someone trying to destroy a small business. Especially not the business where he *worked*. Weston might not find his job incredibly fulfilling, but it paid decently, and he had health coverage and a reasonable amount of holiday time. He couldn't really ask for more than that.

"So," Henry continued, clearly getting the idea that the topic of Sidney was done with. "Tell me again about this fantasy porn that you wrote because you secretly want to bang me."

# Chapter Three

—+——+——+——+——+——+——+——+——+——+——+——+—

HE AWOKE.

He didn't open his eyes right away. The smell of burning wood hit his nose. People were talking in low, worried tones. Others were shouting.

Screaming.

"WingBlade!"

He twitched his fingers, curled them in toward his palm. Opened his eyes. The sky was sapphire blue above him, the twin suns at their zenith.

"WingBlade, get up! We don't have time to be sittin' around on our keisters!"

WingBlade? That didn't sound right, he thought. The twin suns didn't look right, either. And what was all that screaming?

With a groan, he hauled himself into a sitting position, moving one hand to his chest as it throbbed in pain. "What—" he started, grimaced, and then continued, "what happened?"

A face swam into his vision. Ruddy cheeks and a thick braided beard. "Oh, thank the gods," the face said. "Come on, lad, no time to be lyin' around." He took a hand that was offered to him, and climbed to his feet.

He wasn't thinking clearly, he knew that much. Everything seemed so strange and unfamiliar, but *too* familiar at the same time. The last thing he remembered was... he'd been working? Drinking from a mug. He'd put his head down on his desk and closed his eyes.

"Where...?" He looked around, but he didn't see the man. He looked *down*, and oh, there he was. Recognition sparked. "HardIron?"

The dwarf narrowed his eyes at him. "Aye," he said slowly. "That's me. Don't tell me you've also gone and forgotten yourself? That was a mighty crack that dragon dealt you. I thought you'd be sleepin' all winter." He shook his head, and HardIron continued, "You're WingBlade, you fool! One of the DragonSpeakers, and there's a flamin' great dragon tearin' up that yonder village, so get to it!"

HardIron gave him a hard shove, and WingBlade found himself stumbling in the direction of the village. Made of wood and thatched roofs, the buildings were an inferno in the wake of dragon breath. People ran for their lives as bright orange flame licked at their heels, blackening the yellowed grass. The town of Arandin was burning.

And above it all, a colossal red dragon circled in the sky, its roars making WingBlade's ears ring.

His footing steadied as he shook off the sense of panic. WingBlade could now barely recall what he'd been thinking about as he'd awoken; it had likely been delirium, strange dreams confusing him as he lay unconscious.

WingBlade reached for his sword, then unsheathed it from the scabbard that sat diagonally across his back. Long and slender, the blade gleamed a soft silver in the noon sun. Worn black leather wound around the grip, and on the cross guard curled a pair of metal wings that curved up to embrace the sword. The blade that had been given to him when he was but ten winters old, the weapon that had given him his name, as was the custom of all warriors.

Yes, he remembered who he was now. He was WingBlade, the DragonSpeaker of the Eastern Crags. Born to the peasants Fieran and Amona, he had a great destiny, a keen sword, and a strong will.

"Dragon," he shouted, walking bravely into the middle of the burning village. "Come down from your flight! We shall speak about this like equals! We—ow!" A swift kick in the shin had WingBlade taking a step back, glaring down at his dwarf companion. "What was that for, HardIron? I was about to calm the beast and save the village."

"Are you out of your mind?" HardIron snapped at him. "I brought you here to help the *villagers*, you daft rockhead. You've been DragonSpeaker for but a day!"

WingBlade's confidence faltered. "But then... who will Speak?" he asked.

"'Tis SilverEdge's job. You know, the great Speaker from the Southern Tundra?" HardIron looked at him as though WingBlade had lost his wits.

WingBlade lowered his sword as embarrassment crept over him. "I apologize," he said haltingly. "I must have hit my head harder than I thought. I thought I had a shining destiny."

HardIron barked out a laugh, grabbing WingBlade's hand and hauling him out from the middle of the town. "A shinin' example of ego," he agreed cheerfully. "Come now, lad, we'll wait for SilverEdge to show up, and in the meantime, we'll help these villagers. Looks like the dragon's done for the day."

Indeed, the dragon was currently curled on top of the watchtower, watching them all with eyes that burned like the fire licking at its nostrils. It seemed content to rest, its tail idly looped around the deck of the wooden structure. The villagers were gathered by the nearby woods. "One of these days, we're really going to have to stop building with flammable materials, considering how often dragons come around," WingBlade heard one of them say to muttered agreement from the men and women around him.

Together, WingBlade and HardIron worked to help get the villagers ready for travel. Arandin had been destroyed and would take some time to recover; the village elder had called for them to move to the nearest town over for the night. "Why are the peoples of Arandin so calm?" WingBlade muttered to the dwarf, baffled at what he was seeing.

"They're used to it, Wing," HardIron said. He grunted as he helped heft a pile of scrap metal into a cart. "Bloody dragons. They're like pests round these parts. Lot rarer up East, of course."

"Pests," WingBlade repeated. "Massive, flame-breathing, people-eating pests?"

HardIron snorted. "Is that what they're teachin' at the Obsidian Tower these days? No, lad, they've lost their appetite for people. The old Speaker of the West said that dragons don't like eatin' people 'cause we're too bony these days. Not enough food to go around for us lot. Apparently makes us like skinny rabbits or the tiny fish that throw themselves into your net. Not worth botherin' with."

"Oh," WingBlade said faintly.

What had happened to the stories of the great dragons of old? He was sure he remembered dragons being beasts of myth and legend, powerful and beautiful. Ancient, and wise because of it, but terribly deadly, and so far above people that those with soft skin and two legs were seen as little more than snacks.

Was his mistaken assumption because of the hit to his head? No, perhaps he had been afflicted with a witch's spell. Yes, that must be it. All of this very strange not-knowledge must be from a disgruntled witch attempting to confuse him.

"I apologize, my friend." WingBlade dusted off his gloves, taking a step back to avoid the path of a horse and his rider. "My mind is true now. I have been having very strange glimpses of false memory." He rubbed a hand over the back of his neck, smiling ruefully. "I thought I was some great predestined warrior born to battle the fearsome dragons and... don't *laugh*, dwarf, it's not that amusing!"

"Humor of the dwarves, Wing," HardIron replied, mirth still shining in his eyes. "Humor of the dwarves. You lot and your heads in the clouds with your egos to match. Tell you what, lad—once we're done with showin' you around the Flatlands, I'll take you back to my city, and you can learn a bit from how humble we dwarves are."

"*Humble?*" WingBlade protested, grinning. "Humble, he says? Is this from the same HardIron that once boasted, for three days in a row, that he'd caught the biggest fish anybody had ever laid eyes upon?"

The dwarf prodded a finger into WingBlade's chest, his expression stern. "That *was* the biggest fish anybody had ever laid eyes upon," HardIron insisted. "'Twas so big it didn't fit on my father's dining table!"

"Well." WingBlade paused solemnly. "Your family's furniture *is* very small."

There were few options when a dwarf was chasing you with an axe; WingBlade chose to run.

He laughed as he did, darting behind boulders sunken into yellow grass, shouting behind him to HardIron that the dwarf and his short legs would never catch up. After having spent years training in the Obsidian Tower, WingBlade felt like the friendly chase was his freedom from dusty books and nagging professors. He grinned into the wind, his boots pounding against the ground as he ran yet faster, grumpy yelling following him. As he doubled back toward the gathering of the people of Arandin, he caught sight of a figure approaching in the distance, a lone silhouette against blue and gold.

He stopped so fast that HardIron nearly ran into him. "You bloody whelp," HardIron panted, but his grumblings were cut short as he, too, saw the figure. "Oh, it's about time. That'll be SilverEdge, come to Speak."

WingBlade raised a hand to shield his eyes from the glare of the sun in an attempt to see better. As SilverEdge walked closer, WingBlade could pick out spare details about him—a finely wrought black tunic covering dark-gray trousers, the gleam of a silver shoulder guard. The man himself was more than forty winters but seemed hardy and strong despite a weathered face. He had stern blue eyes set in tanned skin. WingBlade suppressed a flutter of excitement. SilverEdge was a legend even among DragonSpeakers after killing the great dragon Telethar in his first year of duty.

"Speaker SilverEdge," WingBlade greeted formally, raising his fist to clasp it over his heart and ducking his head in a respectful bow. Beside him, HardIron did the same. "Your presence is most welcome."

The DragonSpeaker narrowed his eyes at them and looked beyond them to the gathered people. Then he studied the red shape of the dragon in the distance. WingBlade wondered what was going through the man's mind. Was he planning his strategic attack? Was he recalling his long and grand history of dealing with dragons, using his experience to formulate a plan?

SilverEdge drew a deep breath. "Well, looks like a shoo-away job," he said, sounding exasperated.

WingBlade blinked at him. "A shoo-away job?"

"Indeed." The man raised an eyebrow at WingBlade. "That one's young. Hasn't even grown up eating people, and I doubt he ever will. See how the edges of his scales aren't dark? Look, boy, see for yourself."

WingBlade dutifully turned. He could indeed see that the dragon's scales were all red. The older dragons, the ones that had been around before the famine, had dark linings on their scales. Nobody knew why, but the theory was they turned that color after the dragon took a human life.

"But," WingBlade said, dumbfounded, "I thought all dragons were evil and should be slain."

"What was I tellin' you earlier," HardIron grumped. "No offense, Speaker SilverEdge, but I think that Tower is teachin' with old men out of older books. Dragons aren't much more than pests now, whelp. They turn up as they please, and they might not eat people anymore, but they sure do like burnin' up towns when they got nothin' else to do."

SilverEdge's smile barely twitched at the corner of his lips. "Your dwarf friend is right, young Speaker. No longer are the days of glorious battle with flame-breathing foes. Now we truly live up to the title of *Speaker*, in a much more literal way than I think was ever intended."

WingBlade fought to wipe the mystified, disappointed expression off his face. "So we just talk to them now. We tell them to go away and that's our job?"

The amusement in SilverEdge's expression answered his question well enough. Without further dallying, the DragonSpeaker walked toward the still-burning town of Arandin, his gloved hand resting lightly on the pommel of his sheathed blade. Despite everything that he'd just been told, WingBlade couldn't help but think him a heroic figure, striding into danger to confront the mightiest of beasts, framed in flame and shadow.

Five minutes later, instead of watching SilverEdge work, WingBlade found himself ushered off to the nearby river to get water. As if he was little more than a working boy.

He'd muttered under his breath about not getting to see the DragonSpeaker of the Southern Tundra at work. HardIron had given him a swift kick and told him to make himself useful.

WingBlade despondently plopped himself down on a smooth rock near the river. The town was too far away now for him to see properly, partially hidden by a great stone statue close by. The carved face of WolfArrow of the Flatlands seemed to stare down at him, seeing right through him and judging him accordingly. WolfArrow had been a DragonSpeaker from the town of Arandin. He had been a mere boy when he'd traveled to the Tower, guided there by dreams that told him of his fate.

Young children who wanted to grow up to be DragonSpeakers these days were told of the legends of WolfArrow and his healer companion, Silyn; of great women who fought the dragons in ages past, SwanDagger and GrayPike; and of their loyal friends who battled by their sides. BlackLance the Fearless and his single-handed defeat of four dragons, one after the other. StarMaul and the fifty-day quest to find the most elusive dragon of the Red Sweeps.

Ever since he could remember, WingBlade had wanted to be one of them. With his friends, he had pretended he was one of the brave DragonSpeakers and they the dastardly dragons he had to catch. His parents had supported him in his passion, their encouragement endless.

The day he'd arrived at the Obsidian Tower was one of the proudest of his life. WingBlade had studied hard, sparred with trainers at every opportunity.

And now he'd found out that DragonSpeakers vanquished their foes by *talking*.

Heaving a sigh, WingBlade pushed himself to his feet. He supposed there was no use moping about, as that would hardly help anything, and he was going to be needed when the people of Arandin started their journey. He ducked down to the river to fill a bucket but paused when a reflection of a dark shape passed across the water.

A dragon in flight was remarkably quiet. A dragon *landing* was an entirely different matter.

The red dragon landed with an almighty thump on the other edge of the river, and WingBlade yelped in surprise, stumbling backward, sloshing the water over his boots as he dropped the bucket. "Don't eat me," he cried, fumbling for his sword. Years in training and when it came to the real thing, his hands shook. "I know I have some decent muscle on me, but I promise I wouldn't make a very good meal!"

The dragon seemed to regard him with amusement. Its head was as big as WingBlade's body, and it towered over him, seeming to block out the sun. The scales on its body gleamed a pure red, no darkening around the edge, a color as bright as—

A shirt.

Someone had been wearing a shirt that exact same color. Someone WingBlade had also thought was out to get him.

Whispers rushed through the back of his mind. Rumors. A vision of dark eyes and dusky skin, a surprising smile.

WingBlade shook his head hard, trying to dislodge the strange thoughts. The dragon blinked lazily at him, its massive jaw opening to purr out a growl.

Wait. No, not a growl. There were words in that rumble. WingBlade struggled to recall his teachings, the way his elders at the Tower had taught him to truly *listen* to the tone of a dragon's sounds. They did not communicate in mere roars and growls and grunts. There was a language there, one that only DragonSpeakers were taught—but had generally had no use for while killing the dragon.

The dragon repeated what it had said, and WingBlade brightened despite his fear. "I think I understood half of that," he announced. "Something about easy meals?"

That took a moment to sink in.

"Ah." WingBlade took a step back. "Well, you see, I'm told your kind generally *don't* eat people these days. It really would be supremely nice of you if you didn't."

The dragon huffed, tipping its chin up in what looked like a sign of exasperation, and rumbled out another sound. But WingBlade missed it, distracted by the sound of a shout not far away, the sight of SilverEdge walking closer. The man had his blade drawn. Perhaps it had not taken much to convince SilverEdge to kill a young dragon with no blood on its fangs. "Wait!" he called to SilverEdge, holding up a hand to halt him. "Let me talk to it first."

He turned back to the dragon. "I apologize. Could you repeat what you said?"

As the dragon did, WingBlade closed his eyes for a few moments, trying to block out every other noise.

That little rasp at the end, the slight pause between noises—it all had meaning. Humans would never understand the dragontongue as well as dragons, but they could fare well enough.

The dragon had just apologized for scaring the people of the town, though it had joked about them being easy meals.

WingBlade took a moment to process that. He'd never heard of a dragon *joking*; he'd never even thought they might have a sense of humor. Already this dragon was vastly different from the dragons WingBlade had learned about in the Tower. He'd been led to believe they were fierce and wise, though utterly ruthless and uncaring of the people in what the dragons considered their own lands.

The dragon spoke again, a rolling rumble with a little click at the end for a question. "Do you understand me?"

"Somewhat." WingBlade realized he'd had a death grip around the handle of his sword. Slowly, he released the hilt, darting a look to check where SilverEdge was. The man was still a distance away, watching them cautiously.

Then the dragon did something incredible.

It *changed*. Scales rippled over its back like a wave, and in one smooth blur of motion, there was a man standing where the dragon had been. A man with dark eyes that looked so familiar to WingBlade, though he couldn't immediately place his face. Dark-red tattoos coiled over tanned arms, graced the skin in short marks below the man's eyes. He was nearly naked, wearing only a wrap of long scaled material hanging from his hips.

"You couldn't pronounce my real name," the dragon said, teeth glinting white in a savage grin, "so you may call me Sentry, for that is who I am."

"Sentry," WingBlade said dumbly. He'd heard SilverEdge curse in surprise at the change, and he wondered if the DragonSpeaker had ever seen anything of the like. "You look human."

Sentry cocked his head. It reminded WingBlade of the movement that hawks made, a sharp, inquisitive motion. "But I am not. Does this form surprise you?"

"Quite a bit," WingBlade admitted. The most surprising thing about it was that Sentry, the *dragon*, was stunningly attractive. WingBlade had never considered dragons to be attractive before—beautiful, yes, and gorgeously deadly, but not on a human level. Not in any way he could find truly appealing.

But there was the dragon, all long, muscled limbs and catlike eyes, wide and oval with an exotic tilt at the corner. Sentry stepped closer, the river winding around his ankles, moving with an animal grace, a confidence that gave him strength.

"I took this form to better speak to your villager friends in your common tongue," Sentry said. The dragon reached WingBlade's side of the river, affording WingBlade a closer look at him. Now he could see two small horns nestled in Sentry's hair, nearly hidden, and golden jewelry wrapped around his wrists. "I wish to apologize for my behavior."

That got WingBlade's attention. He tore his gaze away from where it had settled, somewhere on Sentry's smooth collarbones, and looked up to his face. "You want to apologize?" he asked suspiciously.

"Yes." Sentry looked regretful. "I had recently talked to my brother and I was in a bit of a temper. I wasn't truly thinking when I burned the town."

That was how WingBlade found himself guiding the dragon through the sparse forest on the edge of the Flatlands, walking toward the assembled villagers. Young and old alike were getting ready to move, and the village elder was moving down the line of people, checking that they would be able to carry what they had brought.

It started with a mule. Its nostrils flared as it caught the scent of the dragon, and it whined in anxiety, the whites in its eyes showing. A man nearby grabbed the donkey's saddle, stopping it from bolting. The man looked over and sucked in a sharp breath at the sight of Sentry. From person to person, the surprise spread, rippling through the crowd and leaving them nervous.

The villagers went still. A hundred men and women stared at them with pale faces. Even HardIron, who had proclaimed dragons to be mere pests, looked on in trepidation. Pests though dragons might be, they were still dangerous.

Sentry stood his ground, calm in the face of the reactions to him. "People of Arandin," he called, "I stand here before you to apologize."

A young woman in the middle of the crowd broke the silence first. "Apologize?" She sounded angry, her lips turned downward in a fierce glare. "You think that will do any good? You burnt our homes to the ground!"

"My son was nearly killed," a man joined in, clutching a young boy to his side. "He was sleeping when our home burned, and I was out in the fields."

"You destroyed my weaving!"

"My cattle ran off because of you!"

"Friends!" WingBlade bellowed, raising his hands in attempt to calm the crowd. "Let the dragon speak!"

He looked at Sentry, giving him an encouraging smile. The dragon did not smile in return, but there was a warmth in his eyes. "I know I cannot magically bring your homes back with words, but I hope—"

A piece of apple hit him in the jaw and clung there for a moment before sliding off and falling to the ground. The villager who had thrown it looked ready to raise his arm again. "Pest!" the man growled, a shovel in his hand as he strode forward. "Your kind are nothing but vermin, dragon, and I shall see to it that there is one less in the world. Starting with you!"

The villager swung the shovel, but it never met its target— WingBlade met it with his sword, metal striking against wood. "There shall be no harm come to this dragon, villager," WingBlade said, his voice unyielding. "He has apologized, and I believe he was about to offer to help rebuild the town."

"Speaker WingBlade, what are you doing?" SilverEdge snapped the words as he walked forward, his own blade held loosely at his side, ready to strike.

"You said it yourself, revered Speaker. We do not kill dragons now." WingBlade lowered his sword, squaring his shoulders. At his side, Sentry had taken a step back, wary. "Were this a court, then Sentry would have a fair trial for the destruction of property."

"There is no court anymore, boy," SilverEdge said harshly. "The famine and poverty have seen to that. There are no lawmen to judge the cases, no spare food to give the prisoners. And we have not killed dragons for many a year because they usually fly off after we speak to them. They do not"—he cast a venomous look at Sentry—"loiter around to rub their gleeful destruction in our faces."

"I would help to rebuild, as the Speaker said," Sentry replied, low and urgent. "See reason, Speaker. I—"

It was not fruit that hit Sentry then—it was a scrap of metal that cut into the side of his jaw. The dragon grunted in pain, and the crowd seemed to go still again as he carefully reached upward to touch his fingertips to the blood.

The crowd surged forward. "Monster," they cried. "Pest! Vermin!"

WingBlade grabbed Sentry around the shoulders, turned him, and hauled him into a run.

Despite going barefoot, Sentry was surprisingly swift, and WingBlade struggled to keep up with him. He flattened yellow grass underneath his boots, the sound of his own breath loud in his ears, and then there was a nudge to his side, the dizzying sensation of being picked up.

And he was flying.

The ground seemed to push downward, shrinking. WingBlade felt cool scales under his hands, and he realized he was on the dragon's back. He hadn't even seen him change.

Massive wings flapped on either side of him, the wind they pushed back buffeting him from all sides. WingBlade laughed, an incredulous noise, as he twisted his head around to watch the villagers grow smaller in his vision, smaller still, until they were little more than dark dots against the golden stretch of the Flatlands.

"Why did you fight for me?" Sentry turned his enormous head to look at WingBlade with one burning eye as he flew. He spoke once more in dragontongue, a trembling hiss.

"I was raised with stories of dragons as murderous beasts," WingBlade admitted, shouting to be heard. "You don't seem like that. You surprised me."

If dragons could be said to smile, then Sentry did so. "You as well, human."

WingBlade laughed again, tipping his face into the wind, feeling his hair blow about him. It was the most free he'd ever felt, up here surrounded by nothing but the sky and the winged creatures. How incredible it must be to be able to fly all the time. And how much of a curse to be assumed a monster when you were not.

—◆— —◆— —◆— —◆— —◆— —◆— —◆— —◆— —◆— —◆— —◆—

# Chapter Four

WHEN Weston awoke, it was to the blunt pressure of a pen poking him in the shoulder. He grunted, cracked open his eyes, and lifted his head from the desk.

"Sentry!" he blurted.

"Close," Sidney said slowly, eyebrows raised in obvious bemusement. "But not quite. It starts with the same letter, I'll give you that much."

Weston fumbled to bat away a Post-it Note that was stuck to his cheek. "I've been asleep for half the day," he said groggily, staring up at Sidney. "Why didn't anybody wake me?"

Sidney frowned at him. "You've only been asleep for five minutes, Weston. I saw you put your head down, and I thought you were just resting your eyes until I saw you drooling. Perhaps you should look into getting more sleep at nighttime, not on your desk."

Blearily, Weston stared at the man as he walked out of his office and disappeared around the corner of the hallway. He could have sworn Sidney was in his dream. That dragon person had looked exactly like him. It hadn't even felt like a dream, either. It had been as real to him as being awake. There'd been a village, and a dwarf, and a dragon, and....

Weston sat upright so quickly he nearly upended his desk. That dream had been *fantastic*! It was everything he wanted to write about, and more besides! There had been a whole world, entire cultures and histories, multifaceted characters. In his rush to grab a pen and spare paper, Weston struggled to recall details, thinking about the Obsidian Tower and the DragonSpeakers. His writing was little more than a messy scrawl as he wrote down what he could remember.

The villagers of Arandin, a hardy people used to scraping a living out of bare rock and grass.

WingBlade, the egotistical DragonSpeaker who was in love with the idea of mystic destinies and great warriors, finding out that perhaps he had some good qualities inside himself that weren't related to the blade.

Sentry, the dragon who was vilified for his very nature.

It was the same setting he'd tried to write about previously, but in his dream it had transformed into something genuine, something tangible and alive. Weston grinned as he read through his notes again, adding details as they came to him.

"What are you grinning about?" Henry said from the doorway.

"I had the most amazing dream!" Weston waved his notes at Henry. "You were there, like I wrote before, as HardIron the dwarf. And I was WingBlade, the DragonSpeaker, and I became friends with a dragon that transformed into a man. It went against both of our natures to make peace, and nobody liked him, but we flew, and it was incredible!"

Henry turned around and walked back out again.

Weston *hmphed* at him and then stared down at his notes once more, excited. This was something he could use. With these notes, maybe he could actually set about writing a real novel.

The rest of the day passed in a blur. Weston finished his design for the puffer fish-slash-squirrel costume and picked out a tablet to order, though he barely thought about it. His mind was too consumed by ideas, glorious *ideas*, that seemed to create themselves and get better all by themselves, as though he wasn't even consciously involved in the making of them. It was intoxicating; he'd never had inspiration like that, and by the end of the day, he had five pages of scribbled notes and a rudimentary map.

As soon as he got home, he eagerly opened his laptop, his fingers hovering over the keys.

And found himself unable to type anything.

A minute ticked by. Weston frowned increasingly harder at the screen.

Five minutes, and he still hadn't typed anything.

"Oh my God," he moaned in despair, burying his face in his hands. "I'm a hack. I'm an ideas man. Everybody hates the ideas man because he can't actually do anything."

No matter how hard he stared at the screen, the words wouldn't come. Weston shuffled his notes, read them through again, but though the images and ideas were clear in his mind, he couldn't translate them into the words of a novel. How did he start it? What was the plot going to be? What growth would the characters go through?

No, he could do this. Weston wasn't going to give up.

He raised his fingers to the keyboard again and very deliberately typed:

—+———+———+——+———+——+———+——+———+——+———+——+——+—

WingBlade was a handsome warrior. The most handsome in all the land.

—+———+———+——+———+——+———+——+———+——+———+——+———+——+—

No. God, no. That wouldn't do. Weston deleted it and started anew.

—+———+———+——+———+——+———+——+———+——+———+——+—

In times of crisis, the people of the Flatlands enjoyed doing activities such as roasting potatoes and cutting them into the colloquially named "fries."

—+———+———+——+———+——+———+——+———+——+——+—

That was even worse and made no sense whatsoever.

Weston glared despondently at his notes. In the corner of the second page, he'd scribbled a little dragon. It reminded him of Sidney. Or, rather, the dragon in his human form had reminded him of Sidney. They looked the same, from the high cheekbones to the gently amused expression. Then again, Weston had once read that people sometimes actually dreamed of blank faces and in their waking moments put familiar faces on those blank spaces. The human mind loved coincidences.

So maybe the dragon hadn't looked like Sidney at all. Perhaps Weston's mind had merely taken one vilified person and likened him to another. Because now that Weston thought about it, there *had* been some strange similarities between Sentry and Sidney, particularly in the way everybody assumed they were evil.

Weston shook his head, trying to clear those thoughts. He was doing a lot of thinking about the company's productivity consultant, and it wasn't even work hours.

"Right," he said, determined, looking back at the screen once more. "Type, man. Just do it."

Maybe he needed to write a small bit of something else, just to get the creative juices flowing. Weston typed.

—◆——◆——◆——◆——◆——◆——◆——◆——◆——◆——◆—

Five people. Two females, three males. All innocent, if you never looked too deep. If you never cared to glance beyond the perfectly made-up appearances and fake smiles so prevalent in the business community, the bright glare of commercialism and customer service hiding the ugliest of flaws.

This was Wickham's job. They were Wickham's job.

"Detective Wickham." A voice roused him out of his watchful silence. Wickham glanced up to see his partner, Saunders. This was a dangerous business, and Wickham had to have somebody to watch his back. "Coffee?"

"No, thanks," Wickham said brusquely, keeping his eye on the oldest of the men. "I have an important job to do. I must uphold the law. I am the cold, iron fist of justice."

Two females. Three males. A jewelry heist with more than one criminal.

Adjusting his fedora, he stood, keeping the brim of the hat low over his eyes. Wickham's heavy trench coat was silent in the wind as he took his Smith & Wesson .38 Special out of the holster, the gun gleaming silver with righteousness in the low light. He might have had a partner, but his gun was the only thing he really trusted.

The cherry of his cigarette glowed red in the dark alley. Wickham ignored the rain beating down on his fedora and staunchly stood his ground.

"You should really get out of the rain." Two feet to his left, Saunders waited under an overhang, perfectly dry. "I know you have some weird addiction to looking manly and skulking around in the shadows, but you'll get pneumonia."

"I'm above pneumonia," Wickham rasped. "I am the law."

He turned toward a nonexistent camera. "It's a cold, rainy night here in the Bronx, but I can see everything. Though I'm supposed to be watching the store front of Pendleton Jewelry, part of me suspects that this whole chaotic case may have started within my own detective agency."

Saunders gave Wickham a strange look. "Detective, you do realize that I can hear you?"

"Though film noir is classically composed for the film setting, I am breaking expectations by creating literary noir," Wickham said coldly. "Do not interrupt me."

-+--+--+--+--+--+--+--+--+--+--+-

It was crap, and Weston knew it, but it had gotten him writing. After all, the key to discipline was to do *something*, right? Now that he'd loosened himself up and gotten over the nervousness of starting a whole novel, Weston was sure he'd be able to write the saga of WingBlade and Sentry.

He poised his fingers over the keys again, excited.

The clock ticked in the background.

With a loud curse Weston would deny was anything less than cool and composed, he gave up and went to bed.

THE next morning, Weston decided the weather was appropriately gloomy, exactly fitting his mood as he trudged into work. It wasn't raining, but the clouds were dark and overcast, a storm heading in on the horizon.

He was still irritated that he hadn't been able to write down his fantasy idea, but perhaps he'd be able to do it tonight. Maybe he just needed some time away from the mad rush of ideas to let them settle a bit.

An enthusiastic e-mail from Mr. Kent greeted him, saying that his puffer fish-squirrel concept design was everything he'd wanted. Weston came close to smiling as he read the e-mail—until he got to the last paragraph, in which Mr. Kent detailed how he wanted to be able to pull a string on the costume and have it puff up, just like a real puffer fish.

Weston had once read that hitting one's head against a solid object burned 150 calories an hour. Maybe if he kept it up for another fifty-nine minutes, he might work off that chocolate bar he'd had last week.

"That doesn't look fun" came Sidney's remark from the doorway. "Bad day already?"

"I hate clients," Weston mumbled against his desk. "I hate *people*. Why didn't I just get a job in the middle of nowhere tending to goats? I wouldn't have to deal with people then."

He heard Sidney laugh. "Yes, but then you'd have to deal with goats, and they try to eat everything."

Weston raised his head from his desk, feeling faintly guilty that he'd been caught taking out his frustration on his forehead. Or the desk. Whichever was softer. "Did you need something?" He attempted to sound politely inquiring. After all, Sidney might look like the drop-dead handsome man-slash-dragon of his ideas, but they were two completely different people. And the one in front of him was a dreaded productivity consultant.

Sidney's easy smile dimmed slightly. "I did, in fact. I was wondering if you'd like to join me for lunch."

That caught Weston by surprise. "This isn't related to my job, is it? Please don't tell me you recommended to Sanderson that he should fire me and he told you to do it so that I don't hate him."

"Your logic cycles are fascinating," Sidney replied, idly amused. "But no, it's not that. It *is* regarding the business, but I'm hardly here to pass on the message of you being fired."

"Oh." Weston had no idea what it might be about, then. "Sure, okay. I'll take my lunch at noon; does that work?"

"Yes, that's perfect." Sidney glanced at his watch. A small, venomous part of Weston was surprised the thing wasn't a Rolex, from the piles of money Sidney must surely rake in from shutting down small businesses left and right. "I'll come by then."

Spending the next few hours being slightly paranoid was not fun and also not very good for Weston's productivity levels. He kept wondering if Sidney wanted to talk to him about the tablet—had he not ordered the right one? He was sure Sidney had said that it was up to him to choose, but Weston dreaded the discussion so much he couldn't help thinking in circles.

His paranoia didn't get any better when he stood up at his desk to get a better view of the commotion going on outside his office. Aiko looked furious. Henry was scowling. Mary, whom everyone called "the office mother," looked near tears. Moran, a constantly bedraggled-looking man, seemed close to tearing his hair out.

Whatever had happened, it wasn't good. Weston took the few steps necessary to make it outside his office and asked, "What's happening?"

"The Leech is saying he's going to recommend job cuts."

"I might lose my job!"

"I've been working here for ten years. I can't lose this job!"

All of the answers came at once, leaving Weston reeling. "Wait, did he say which jobs?"

"Whichever they are, they'd better not be mine," Moran said.

Henry made an odd little growling sound in the back of his throat. "No, he didn't say which jobs. Just 'some'. He said he thought it might be necessary."

Weston hated to point out logic in a chaotic situation, he really did. When a group of people who were angry about something got together, they seemed to revel in their anger, happily wallowing in it and feeding more fuel to the fire. He still felt the need to say, "'Might be necessary' is pretty different than 'going to recommend', guys."

"So? He still used the words 'job cuts'," Aiko hissed. "You don't do that."

"It's like blasphemy," Henry agreed. "Thou shalt not take the name of Job Cuts in vain. And I can't believe you're defending the guy, Weston. You were doing that yesterday morning too."

Weston folded his arms across his chest, feeling defensive. "He's not *that* bad," he insisted. "Okay, productivity consultant, kind of weird and seems to have no real social life to speak of." Not that he could really judge. He didn't have much of one either. "But that doesn't make him a bad person, and—"

"Weston."

They all went quiet. Aiko awkwardly shuffled her feet. The appearance of Sidney seemed to have shocked—or embarrassed— everybody into silence.

"Lunch?" Sidney gave Weston a smile that was on the bland side, making Weston indulge in paranoia again. Had Sidney heard Henry and Aiko's conversation? Or, even worse, Weston's description of him as "kind of weird"?

"Yeah. Let me just grab my wallet," Weston managed and scuttled into his office, his shoulders hunched. By the time he emerged again, the group had scattered to the far corners of the building, though he could see Henry glaring at Sidney's back.

They exited the building out onto the busy road, the walk mostly silent save for the occasional small talk about where they should go for lunch. Weston felt more awkward by the minute, completely sure that Sidney was unhappy with him and was only doing this because he'd promised earlier.

In a sharp contrast to Weston's hesitant steps to avoid the moving crowd on the street, Sidney's stride was much more confident, making Weston pick up his pace to keep up. They chose a small corner café that boasted an all-day breakfast and some of the best coffee in town.

They picked a table, and Sidney unhooked his messenger bag from over his shoulder and set it on the ground. Only when Weston caught an accidental glimpse of its contents did he say something that wasn't lunch related. "Is that *Lord of the Flies* in your bag?"

Sidney looked briefly startled, but an abashed smile crossed his lips. "I reread it occasionally."

"I'm more of a Tolkien guy myself," Weston replied.

"Is it the three-page-long ramblings about a made-up language?" Sidney's smile turned sly. "Or the five-paragraph environment descriptions?"

Weston put on an insulted expression. "It's better than pig heads and young boys running around killing each other. I had to read that in school; I think it traumatized me."

"It's always about the pig head when someone doesn't like the novel," Sidney sighed dramatically. "I thought someone like you would like *Lord of the Flies*."

Weston wasn't sure if he should be insulted or not, mostly because he had no idea what Sidney meant by that. "Someone like me?" He hesitated. "What, do I give off the air of secretly being a murderer?"

Sidney laughed, shaking his head. "No, no, of course not. I meant an aspiring author. I'm sorry, I saw a glimpse of your notes when you practically dashed out of work yesterday. You looked excited."

"I was." Weston slumped in his chair. "And yeah, I try to write. It never really happens, though."

Just the reminder was depressing enough. But not depressing enough for him to miss the fact he and Sidney were having what one might call a "real person" conversation. It wasn't small talk about the weather or talk directly related to business. Sidney, far from the business rumors, was beginning to seem as though he might be engaging and interesting to talk to.

Weston could hear a little Henry voice in the back of his mind, shouting *blasphemy* at him.

"That must be frustrating," Sidney said. He waved over a waitress as soon as he saw one free and ordered coffee and food for himself. Weston did the same—a mochacchino, since he might as well try something a bit different after already having coffee that morning, and a panini.

"Yeah, it is. I just have all these ideas, but I can never write them down." Weston huffed, giving a rueful smile. "Actually, everything comes out a commentary on the stereotypes of the genre I'm going for. Maybe I'm destined to be a critic instead."

"Oh? What kind of commentary?" Sidney looked interested, leaning forward slightly. Weston didn't know why he took particular notice of it, but he couldn't help staring for a few seconds longer at the way Sidney had shifted into the sunlight, which highlighted his dark eyes into a rich brown.

He really was unfairly attractive for a productivity consultant.

"The kind where all my characters do is have dialogue about common clichés." Weston fiddled with a napkin, tearing off the corners. His paranoia was fading—surely if Sidney was going to give him horrible news, he wouldn't engage Weston in conversation like this—but nervousness still lingered in his thoughts. "Like how in detective novels it always seems to be raining, and the main character sounds like he gargles gravel."

Sidney chuckled. "Maybe you're just worried about falling into those stereotypes?"

That made sense, somewhat. "I just want to write something *unique*," Weston sighed. "Something that makes people think. I don't think I'm ever going to be one of the great authors of history, but I'd like to do something interesting, you know? Not the same old stuff that gets put out every year."

"That's what a lot of people like, though," Sidney pointed out. "It's reassuring to know how a story ends or how a character is going to behave. In a way it's like reading a favorite book all over again."

"I guess." Weston knew he sounded rather reluctant. Whether it was because of what he wanted to achieve as a writer or because that Henry voice was screaming at him never to agree with the Leech about anything, he wasn't sure.

They fell into a surprisingly nonawkward silence as they waited for their orders. Well, Weston thought it might have been comfortable on Sidney's end. For him, the whole "okay with not talking" thing lasted about two minutes, long enough for him to mentally bring up and discard every potential conversational topic. Then it did get awkward. Desperate not to do something weird like stare at Sidney, he latched his gaze onto a poster just over Sidney's right shoulder. It advertised a band Weston had no interest in seeing, but since he needed something to do, he read through the list of venues and dates.

Their food and coffee came out, and Weston started on the panini he'd ordered, trying to eat as neatly as he could. He'd been told he was a messy eater, and it wouldn't do to stuff his face in front of somebody who could recommend that he be fired.

"I suppose," Sidney said eventually, "that you're wondering why I asked you out to lunch."

Everything in Weston wanted to shout *yes, for the love of God, tell me so that I don't have to keep mentally clutching my pearls.* Instead, very calmly, he said, "I was wondering that, yes."

Sidney's expression turned faintly embarrassed, and he didn't answer for a few moments. He seemed to be struggling with what to say. "I'm aware that there's a good deal of rumors flying around about me. That I'm strange or weird or too quiet. That I'm attempting to shut down Sanderson Designs."

"Oh, no, they don't think all of that," Weston hedged. It was a complete lie. His coworkers thought all of that and worse. Weston thought a few of those things himself.

"Yes, they do." Sidney's smile was so faint that Weston almost missed it, the expression more perfunctory than genuine. "The walls in those offices aren't well soundproofed."

Ah, shit. That meant Sidney had probably heard some of what Weston had said about him. Granted, Weston hadn't gotten as verbally nasty as Henry or Aiko, but he'd still contributed. Office rumors were a strange form of peer pressure; if you didn't agree with the consensus of opinion, you were deemed equally strange.

He hadn't thought anything about it at the time, but now, seeing Sidney's reaction to it, Weston started to feel a little bad. He'd never meant to hurt the guy.

"I just wanted…." Sidney trailed off with a sigh. "I invited you to lunch because I just wanted *someone* in the office to not hate me."

Now Weston felt *really* bad.

"It's not that we hate you," Weston tried to reassure him. "Okay, *I* don't hate you. We're all just kind of terrified that you might recommend to our boss that he cut half our jobs. I mean, you saw how everybody got just before. We like our jobs and we don't want to lose them."

"I'd never recommend job cuts if they weren't necessary," Sidney said. Which wasn't exactly reassuring. He looked as though he wanted to say more, but he didn't, sipping at his coffee instead.

The man confused Weston. Taken at face value, he seemed coldly reserved most of the time and not all that great at conversations about work. So far he'd shown flashes of a person underneath—teasing Weston about his reluctance about the tablet, the way he'd been interested in talking about books—but those were only two instances.

"I don't hate you," Weston repeated. "Really."

Then again, this *was* the first time he'd seen Sidney outside of work.

"Thank you." Sidney's smile was held in the crinkles at the corner of his eyes. "Lukewarm is better than cold, I suppose."

Weston opened his mouth to reply, but he could hardly lie. He didn't feel the warm fuzzies toward Sidney, and it would be wrong and trite of him to go on a diatribe about Sidney's perceived good qualities just to reassure the man.

He closed his mouth again without replying. It wasn't all that subtle, and Sidney obviously saw the hesitation. His expression fell slightly, but Weston thought he did a pretty good job of covering it up.

This was awkward.

"You're... intelligent?" Weston finally ventured.

For a long few moments, Sidney simply stared at him. Then he started laughing, genuinely amused at Weston's effort. And Weston couldn't help but join in, their laughter dissipating the awkward tension between them.

"I'm sorry, that was terrible," Weston said, still grinning. "But I do mean it. I kind of like that you're rereading *Lord of the Flies*. I might prefer rings to flies with my lords, but it's cool."

If Weston had to rate his emotions toward Sidney on a scale between Love and Extremely Uncaring, he'd currently settle in around Tentative Like but with Remaining Suspicions.

Sidney went back to his food with a small smile as his only reply. Weston knew it was probably rude to stare, so he did the same, taking small bites of his panini. It was surprisingly good, so he made a mental note of the café. Now that the awkward silence was broken, it was strangely easy to just have a silent, companionable meal with Sidney.

And after the meal, Weston discovered Sidney was a surprisingly good tipper, though he seemed shy when the waitress thanked him happily. Weston supposed being nice to food service employees was a good character trait to have. He just wasn't sure if it made up for everything else.

"I'M SO worried about my job," Weston miserably told the counter his face was currently on.

It didn't seem particularly sympathetic toward his plight. But then again, that was counters for you. Too wooden—and oh dear, if he was making mental puns, maybe he'd drunk his beer too fast.

Henry, however, patted him on the back. "Well, if we get fired, we'll do something really embarrassing," he consoled. "Like flash our asses out the building windows right as a tour bus full of old grannies comes past."

That did cheer Weston up slightly, so he sat up straight again. After work had ended, Henry had insisted on dragging him out to the nearest bar to have a drink, most likely for the purposes of calming him down after a busy day. Weston had spent three hours trying to figure out how to design a costume that inflated, and Henry, who managed the sewing department, had bemoaned his day of wrestling with obstinate button companies.

Weston favored this kind of bar—none of the loud music or rowdy people that came in typical bars, just a nice, quiet atmosphere with low light and a decent beer on tap. It helped that the bar wasn't particularly popular, sandwiched between a more popular nightclub and a secondhand antique store.

"So how *was* your lunch with the Leech?" Henry didn't bother to try to sound as though he wasn't very interested in prying.

"He was... surprisingly okay," Weston said, shrugging. "We talked a bit about books. He told me he rereads *Lord of the Flies* occasionally."

Henry grimaced. "So he's a psycho too. Awesome."

"What about reading *Lord of the Flies* makes someone a psycho?" Weston laughed. "He said he liked how metaphorical it was."

"That book is all about kids straight-up murdering each other and going nuts on a beach," Henry argued. "And don't they kill that fat kid in the end?"

Weston was too busy laughing to reply right away. "Wrong character, but close. They kill Simon, the personification of peace and connection to nature."

"That's even worse." Henry snorted, holding a finger up to the bartender to order another drink. "The point is, who *enjoys* that shit? It's depressing. I had to read it in school."

Weston couldn't really argue with that. It *was* a depressing book, but that was the point of it, he supposed, to display human nature at its worst.

"Anyway, he said that he wasn't going to recommend firing anybody unless it was absolutely necessary," Weston said, going back to staring at his beer. "But I don't even know what that means. What does absolutely necessary mean? They're losing money for the business? They're not productive? They smell?"

"You'd definitely be up for a recommendation if that last one is true," Henry said sagely.

Weston felt an elbow to Henry's ribs spoke more eloquently than he could with words. "It just freaks me out. Everybody's saying that he's all evil, and then he goes and does things like make me have a nice conversation with him over lunch. And all through this, he could be thinking about telling Sanderson to fire my ass."

"Maybe he's luring you into a false sense of security," Henry replied, though his tone didn't hold as much teasing as it normally did. He was staring down at the counter, his shoulders slumped. "Shit, mine could be one of the first jobs to go. Or at least *I* could go."

"There will never be a better sewing department manager than you, Henry," Weston consoled him, his attempted back pat made a bit clumsy by his beer intake. Maybe he'd order another.

Henry looked hopeful. "Not even at someplace like Gucci?"

"Not even at Gucci." Weston paused, thoughtful. "Although the sewing department manager there probably earns a *lot* more than you."

When he finally staggered his way home two hours and another beer later, Weston wasn't sure if he felt better or worse about his future with Sanderson Designs. He and Henry had reassured each other that they were completely irreplaceable in the business, that nobody would ever be as good at their jobs as they were, and that Sanderson Designs would go down in flames if they ever got fired. But as soon as Weston stepped out of the bar, the cold night air slapped him in the face, taking away his warm, beer-fuelled confidence.

It wasn't that he could never get another job. Weston had decent credentials to his name, and he had some savings tucked away. In the event of losing his job, he knew he could probably get other work in the same area but in a different company. But Weston *liked* Sanderson Designs. He liked that it was a small business that ran itself in a very personal manner; he liked that their boss took them out to the bar on occasion; he liked that it wasn't run like an ultra-cost-efficient machine at the expense of human sanity.

He'd managed to thoroughly depress himself by the time he fumbled his key into his front door. After collapsing onto his couch, Weston dragged his laptop over onto his lap. As the screen blinked on, his latest endeavor in writing popped up on display. As in, there was a document, but it was utterly blank.

Which was somehow even more depressing.

With an aggrieved sigh, Weston turned the television on to use it as white noise in the background as he tipped his head back, thinking of the world he'd dreamed about. Again, his thoughts flashed back to Sentry.

Though he and Sidney did look startlingly similar, Weston was sure he hadn't actually put Sidney in his dream as a misunderstood dragon shape-shifter. The physical resemblance had to be pure coincidence. Except at lunch, Sidney had worn an expression for a few seconds, when he'd admitted that the excursion was for a chance to see if he could have someone at Sanderson Designs not hate him. It had been a mix of embarrassment and hope, a little quirk at the corner of his lips, a slight eyebrow lift.

Sentry had had much the same expression when he'd been trying to apologize to the villagers in Weston's dream—the details of the expression had been different, but the feeling behind it had been alike. It was the same situation too: a man who was perceived as a threat attempting to explain that he was vilified for all the wrong reasons.

Weston knew he shouldn't read too much into dreams. But the memory of that lunch had softened his suspicion toward Sidney somewhat, and the comparison to Sentry—though completely strange and not relevant at all considering it was a dream—only furthered his temptation to tentatively trust the man. Weston liked to think he wasn't too judgmental about people until he had solid evidence, because doing otherwise was more than a little rude.

So he decided he'd try not to be too harsh on Sidney. Everybody deserved a chance, right?

Weston didn't get any writing done that night. As much as he tried, whenever he attempted to call up inspiration by thinking about the dream, his thoughts strayed to Sidney and Sentry. Eventually, irritated at his own uselessness, Weston put the laptop aside. Maybe when Sidney had done his job and was gone from Sanderson Designs, Weston would be able to stop mixing the man up in his writing ideas.

# Chapter Five

THERE was an empty desk where Moran had sat yesterday.

Weston didn't actually notice until his third pass of the place. He'd walked through the IT support desk cluster once for coffee, a second time to talk to Henry, and only on the third time did he vaguely wonder why Moran wasn't at his desk.

"Judy? Is Moran sick?" Weston inquired, frowning down at the desk.

"Not that I know of," she answered. Though Judy's dress sense was smart and proper in a button-up blouse and pencil skirt, the image of office professionalism was somewhat lost on her due to a large amount of dark regrowth in her platinum-blonde-dyed hair, and multiple piercings in her ears. "He's probably hungover. You know him."

Weston snorted into his coffee. "Probably," he agreed. Moran—first name unknown to most people at Sanderson Designs—had the kind of voice that carried throughout the entire office, an enthusiastic rambling that never seemed to let up. Weston enjoyed the man's company because he couldn't really hear him in his own office. He thought Judy might feel differently. "I guess he won't mind me borrowing his stapler, then."

He tugged one of Moran's drawers open. It was empty.

"Huh," Weston said, moving to the other drawers. They were all empty too, save for one that had a lone pencil hidden at the back.

"What 'huh'?" Judy turned her chair around.

"I think Moran might be… kind of gone." Weston stared down at the empty drawer, realization dawning.

Judy leaned over to peer into the drawers, her eyes widening in alarm. "He's been fucking fired," she said, stunned.

A head popped up over the low dividing wall between the tech desks. "Someone's been *fired*?" Another two shocked voices joined the chorus.

"Moran's stuff is gone," Weston attempted to explain. "So either he's dead, or he's been fired." In retrospect, that probably wasn't the best thing to say. "Okay, probably fired. If he'd died yesterday then his stuff wouldn't be gone this quick." *Really* not the best thing to say. "I'm sure he's just been fired! It's okay!"

His attempted reassuring grin apparently didn't do much for the small crowd that had gathered around. Weston awkwardly let the grin slide off his face.

"Okay, where's the Leech?" Aiko's voice came from somewhere at the back of the crowd; news spread fast in small offices.

"He called in," Judy replied. "Said he was sick."

"Sick? Yeah, right," Aiko scoffed, hands on her hips. Weston idly noticed her fingernails were bright green today. "You know what? I bet he called in because *he* recommended Moran be fired, and he doesn't want to face the music."

A sick feeling gathered in the pit of Weston's stomach. Maybe Henry was right. Maybe the lunch Sidney had taken him had been to lure him into a false sense of security. Maybe the whole big deal about the tablet was like a consolation prize: get a tablet, then get fired! But it's okay, because you got a cheap, crappy tablet!

"No, come on," he tried. "He said he wouldn't recommend that unless it was absolutely necessary. And Moran is Sanderson's son's friend; he wouldn't do that."

"Just because small businesses get a bit incestuous, that doesn't mean the Leech wouldn't do it." Judy was shaking her head but already turning back to her computer. Maybe Moran was more annoying to sit next to than Weston initially thought. "I'm just surprised Sanderson *did*. He would have had to approve firing Moran."

In the midst of the rising panic of the gathered group, Weston silently took his leave, heading back to his office. He slumped in his chair, staring blankly at his desk.

A cardboard box sat on it, about the right size for a tablet. And when he opened his e-mail, there was a message from Sidney. It read:

> *I know which model you ordered, but I think you underestimated your own ability and therefore your needs. You deserve the better model.—Sidney Romero*

It should have been a nice gesture. A very small part of Weston's brain, hiding right in the back, did recognize that. But fresh off witnessing a fellow worker get fired, all he could think was, *But that isn't the model I ordered.* He'd wanted the previous one, not the newer one. He'd finally gotten himself to adjust to the idea of a tablet, and he'd wanted *that one*.

It probably wasn't something worth getting too irritated over, but Weston couldn't shake that feeling, no matter how deeply he tried to breathe. Sidney obviously thought he was too stupid to order his own tablet, like Weston was stuck in the Jurassic period and Sidney was the futuristic spaceman arrogantly guiding him to better ways. But he decided he might as well get it over and done with, so he opened the package and went about setting the tablet up, scowling at it every once in a while. It took some getting used to, and over the next hour, Weston had to tell himself not to give up every five minutes.

He didn't like it at first. It felt like trying to draw over glass with an empty pen—and he supposed that was exactly what it was— and he felt lost without the familiar scratch of graphite over paper that dragged at the pencil tip.

Eventually, though, he got the hang of it. He even started liking it, because he really didn't have to break out the eraser every time he made a mistake on a line. All it took was a simple button press to erase the mistake. Weston found himself pleasantly surprised, even smiling on the occasion when he discovered he could do something cool.

Maybe it wasn't as bad as he'd thought—and the model that Sidney had ordered *was* quite a bit bigger than the one Weston had picked out. Maybe Sidney knew what he was doing.

At lunch, he, Henry, Aiko, and Judy went down to the nearest café to have their weekly bitch and gossip. While Aiko and Henry viciously tore into the topic of Sidney, Judy seemed surprisingly reserved. Weston watched her for a moment, expecting her to jump in on the insulting. He ended up nudging her arm with an elbow, sending her a quizzical look.

She gave one right back. "What? I'm not feeling up to the gossip."

"You're always up for gossip," Weston pointed out.

Judy huffed a little laugh. "Not this time. I had a think about it—I don't think the Leech just randomly recommended that Sanderson fire Moran. We might be hell-bent on hating him, but he seems smart."

Weston thought back to the book in Sidney's messenger bag, the brief conversation they'd had about metaphorical text. "He is," he agreed. "But Moran sat next to you. I thought you'd be all up on the hate parade."

"Apparently not." Judy shrugged, sipping at her tea. "Not today, anyway. I was up all night last night making sure my daughter's fever didn't spike too high; I think I'm just too tired."

"Oh, she's sick?" Weston frowned in concern. "Is she okay? I didn't know. Are *you* okay?"

"I'm just tired. Perils of a single mother." Judy laughed quietly. "She's got a bit of the flu."

Weston took a moment to thank Fate—or whoever was up there listening—that he was not a parent. He knew he'd make an absolutely terrible one, what with his predilection for staying up until three in the morning, buzzed on caffeine, trying to write. Or his fondness for collecting tacky antique statues, which would easily break under the force of an energetic child. He didn't know how Judy did it.

"Well, if you need anything, you know you can call me, right? I only live five minutes away," Weston insisted. He and Judy might not be the greatest of friends, but he liked her. She put her head down and got work done, which was always an admirable quality. "If you need, I don't know, food or cold medication. Or someone to stand around so you can laugh at them."

Judy grinned at him, patting his hand. "You're sweet, Weston. Why haven't you got yourself a nice girlfriend yet?"

"Uh." Weston was pretty sure that was obvious, even as he felt a flush rise to his cheeks. "Because I'm gay?"

Judy didn't miss a beat. "Boyfriend, then. Someone nice and steady who can deal with your flailing."

"I don't flail," Weston protested. "I make expansive gestures."

"You flail." Laughing to herself, Judy turned back to her food, picking at a muffin.

Aiko's voice was growing louder in her displeasure, and Weston turned to catch Henry waving a hand at her, trying to get her to speak quieter. Weston had been informed that Aiko did indeed have an indoor voice, but as he'd never heard it, he suspected Henry might be lying about that.

"Guys, we don't *know* that Sidney suggested Moran be fired," he cut in. He could feel Judy's approving expression at his side. "I know it's weird that he's sick on the same day, but sometimes a cigar is just a cigar."

"I have no idea what you mean by that." Henry frowned at him.

"It's Freud," Weston attempted to explain. "You know. Phallic symbolism."

"And *why* are you thinking about phalluses in connection to the Leech?"

"That's not…." Weston gave up. He was surrounded by Philistines. "It's a metaphor. It means that maybe Sidney really is just sick and it's not some big conspiracy to hide from backlash."

"Maybe," Aiko said, though she sounded doubtful. "We should ring him. Or someone should go over to his place and check. Do we know his address?"

"I think finding that out would make us stalkers," Judy pointed out. "A restraining order is not something that I need in my life right now."

"If he comes in tomorrow, he'll probably look kind of not well?" Weston finished the last bite of his panini. "So we can, I don't know, stalk him there. Does it count as not stalking if you're both in the same building anyway?"

Henry muffled a laugh behind his coffee. "I think it still counts."

That was a pity. Weston was curious about this whole thing himself. Though he felt more inclined to have positive feelings toward Sidney right then, the timing between Sidney saying he might recommend some people be fired, and Moran getting fired, seemed to be more than a coincidence. After that lunch and the pleasant conversation, after Sidney upgrading his tablet order, Weston wanted to believe the man was essentially a force for good.

But productivity consultants were still the bane of small businesses.

The rest of their lunch passed by with small talk and another round of drinks—Weston switched to orange juice the second time around, because he didn't think he should approach the second half of his workday hopped up on caffeine. The walk back to work was short and pleasant, Weston having to slow his pace as Henry and Judy insisted on window shopping.

Without the papers stuck everywhere, his office looked disturbingly clean. Professional, almost. It was jarring but nice at the same time, and when Weston sat, he had to smile at the interior of the room, feeling quite pleased with it. What was it people said? A clean environment led to a clean mind?

He dragged his tablet closer and tapped the stylus against the screen to start it up. He'd been in the middle of a design when he'd left for lunch.

It remained blank.

Weston frowned at it and tapped it again. It refused to start up a second time. He glanced at his computer, checking that the design he'd been working on for a few hours was still there—thankfully it was. But the tablet wasn't turning on.

And on his second monitor was the e-mail from Sidney, cheerfully saying he'd ordered a different tablet than the one Weston had wanted.

Weston found himself squinting at it suspiciously. The professional tone and businesslike encouragement seemed to be dry mocking, telling Weston that he wasn't smart enough to pick his own model, so Sidney had done it for him. It seemed to say, *I'm trying to take this small business down one person at a time, so I sent you a malfunctioning tablet.*

No, that had to be *too* paranoid. He was sure that was going too overboard.

But with Moran being fired, Sidney taking a "sick day," and now a failed device that would make Weston lose the rest of the day of work, was he really being too paranoid?

With an irritated growl, Weston scooped the tablet up and made his way to the tech department. Moran's empty desk seemed to smugly taunt him on the way past, like a giant sign saying *you're next.*

"Fix this," Weston demanded, shoving it at the first technician he found.

The man—Weston vaguely remembered his name was Billy—stared blankly at him. Weston had noticed computer technicians did that a lot. "I don't know how to fix tablets, man," Billy drawled, glancing over the device.

"But you're a technician. You can figure it out," Weston said desperately. "It's just like a computer, right?"

Billy's blank expression eased into slight condescending amusement. "Not really. Actually, not at all."

"But I need it fixed!" Weston held the tablet out again, silently pleading Billy to do something about it. "The productivity consultant ordered me a new one, and now it doesn't work, so either I fucked it up somehow and just cost the company a lot of money, or Sidney is sneakily trying to get me fired, and I can't deal with this!"

Maybe Judy did have a point about his flailing.

Billy didn't appear to be sympathetic to Weston's problems, but he did take the tablet with a long-suffering sigh, peering through his glasses at it. He twisted it over in his hands a few times, scratched at his patchy beard, and finally concluded, "You burned it, man."

"What?" Weston narrowly avoided screeching. "I didn't burn it; how could I have burned it?"

"See this cable?" Billy turned the tablet over to show Weston. The black cable looked suspiciously half-melted at its entry point. "It overheated and now the wires don't work, so it's not getting any power."

Weston was thankful that he didn't verbally add the implied *dumbass* on the end of that sentence.

"So I broke it," Weston said numbly. "Or...."

"You said you got this today?" At Weston's nod, Billy tilted his head in curiosity. "It's not impossible to get shit exploding right out of the box, but it's not exactly common, either. Maybe it got wrecked when it was being delivered."

"Or someone sabotaged it."

Weston didn't *want* to think that Sidney would do something like that. It would take a lot of effort for something so small, but it could work, in a very sneaky way. Reduce his productivity, make him cost the company too much money, get him fired.

"Can you fix it?" he continued.

"Sorry, man. You'd need to send it back to the company," Billy said, handing the tablet to Weston, already turning back to the computer he was working on. "I told you, I don't know shit about tablets."

Weston despondently walked back to his office and did not throw the tablet out the window, although he really wanted to. His manager was on holiday for the week, which left Sanderson as the person he would contact to apologize to, but the thought filled him with dread. He was sure he could just work on paper for the rest of the day. And after work, he'd send the stupid tablet in to be fixed.

Then, after he'd done all of that, maybe he'd ring Sidney and inquire just the what the hell the man thought he was up to.

# Chapter
## Six

—+——+——+——+——+——+——+——+——+——+——+——+—

"MR. KENNEDY, do you know what it is that I hold in my hand? This is a fourteen-carat white-gold ring with an inset 0.83 carat European-cut diamond. Do you want to know much it is worth?"

Detective Wickham thrust the ring into the face of Mr. Kennedy, who recoiled, looking askance at the jewelry. So involved was he in the interrogation, Wickham barely noticed the vertigo and a strange sensation of not knowing where or who he was.

He felt as though he'd been somewhere before. An image of a bed flashed across the back of his mind, cold sheets and a strange luminescent device. A "lap top"?

Good God, he was thinking gibberish.

Wickham shook it off, determined to keep his attentions firmly focused on the suspect.

"I'm afraid I do not know how much it is worth, Detective," Mr. Kennedy said, an odd nervousness beginning to show on his face. The man withdrew a handkerchief from his pocket and dabbed at his bulbous forehead. "As I stated before, I was merely at Pendleton Jewelry to look at the shop's wares. I did not see the price tag attached to that particular piece."

"And did you see anybody looking at it?"

"I did not, Detective. Perhaps if you could tell me which area of the shop it was in, it might refresh my memory?"

Mr. Kennedy looked suspiciously uncomfortable. The large man shifted in his seat, mopping his forehead once again, a redness beginning to creep up from under his collar. He wore a top hat perched above thinning hair; his suit jacket was narrow and buttoned high—not a very flattering cut for a man of his size, but it was the fashion of the day. Strangely, he wore one white sock and one black sock.

At the time of the crime in Pendleton Jewelry, Mr. Kennedy, by his own admission, had been perusing the watches in the rightmost section of the shop. Upon entering, he had spoken with the owner of the shop to inquire about the latest models of timepieces that had been delivered. At fifteen minutes past noon, the robber—one Mr. Smith—had entered, promptly demanded everybody lie down on the floor, and stated his intention to rob Pendleton Jewelry.

But Mr. Smith was not the only robber in the shop.

A sharp knock sounded on the door, breaking Wickham's concentration. It looked as though his time with Mr. Kennedy was up.

Detective Saunders was waiting for him in the hallway. "Did you get anything out of Mr. Kennedy?" Saunders asked, checking his watch. Wickham took a second glance at him. He looked strangely familiar. Olive skin, dark eyes....

Well, of course Saunders looked familiar. He was Wickham's partner. Wickham was thinking some very strange things today; perhaps he was coming down with an illness.

"No." Wickham shook his head. "But now we have Ms. La Rue."

They walked to the next room over, where a woman of obvious wealth sat at Wickham's desk. She smiled at them with brightly painted lips, her simple dress at odds with her expensive accessories. "Detectives," Ms. La Rue greeted, waving a gloved hand at them.

"Ms. La Rue," Wickham replied gravely as he took a seat. He was not going to be fooled by her pleasant demeanor.

"Please, call me Juliet."

"I don't think we're nearly well enough acquainted for that, Ms. La Rue, but thank you for the offer," Saunders said, sitting next to Wickham on the other side of the desk. "Now, why don't you tell us your version of the events?"

"I was at Pendleton Jewelry to look for a brooch for the town ball happening next week," Ms. La Rue started. "Oh, I simply *can't* wait for it. Did you know that Charles Chesterton is going to be there? The actor. Imagine, Charles Chesterton coming to our little party!"

"I am sure it will be lovely, ma'am. Did you find a brooch?" Saunders subtly nudged her back in the right conversational direction.

"I am afraid not, Detectives." Ms. La Rue's lips turned downward in a pretty frown. "I was interrupted by the burglar. He came in through the front door and told us all to stick our hands up because he was going to rob the store."

"He told you to stick your hands up?" Wickham jotted a note. Mr. Kennedy had said the burglar had told them to lie on the floor.

"Yes, I am absolutely sure he said that." Ms. La Rue attempted to peer over the desk to see what Wickham was writing.

"And are you aware, Ms. La Rue," Saunders said, "that Mr. Smith used to work for the police force?"

Wickham looked over at Saunders in surprise. He had not known that. He had not spent any time with Mr. Smith as of yet, but as far as Wickham was aware, the man had been escorted to the police station with his face-covering mask still firmly on.

But now that he thought about it, Saunders's previous partner had been named Smith. A man who stood at six foot one, average weight, exactly the build of the Mr. Smith who had been brought in.

"Oh, dear me, I didn't know that!" Ms. La Rue looked positively faint, the blush on her cheeks seeming darker as she went pale. "I did not imagine such a thing possible—our police force, committing a crime!"

Saunders's face was grave. "*Former* police officer," he reminded Ms. La Rue gently in an attempt to calm her hysteria. "Did Mr. Smith speak to you at all?"

"No, not at all." Ms. La Rue seemed to be calming down.

Wickham looked over to see Saunders writing in his notepad. He could make out the words "diamonds" and "emeralds."

"The burglar approached the manager and told him to empty the vault," Ms. La Rue continued. "He then asked specifically for diamonds and emeralds."

A coldness washed over Wickham. How had his partner written down those exact two things *before* Ms. La Rue told him? Wickham knew Saunders hadn't interviewed anybody yet—during Wickham's talk with Mr. Kennedy, Saunders had been filing the paperwork of the arrest.

"He must have said something else," Saunders said, his voice firm. "Just think, ma'am."

Ms. La Rue frowned. "I don't recall that he did."

"He must have!" Saunders cracked the words like a whip. His very being radiated tension, from his shoulders to his white-knuckled grip on his pencil.

The lady startled back, rising from her seat in fear. "Detective Saunders," she gasped, pressing a gloved hand to her chest. "I swear on the law itself that the burglar said no more!"

Saunders rose as well. "Ms. La Rue, if I find out that you are lying to me, I will have you in cuffs as well. You are a suspect in this crime. You were found with a twenty-two-carat gold necklace in your pocket, with the price tag still attached. Do you want to explain that?"

"Saunders, calm down," Wickham said, frowning up at him. He was confused about this sudden aggressiveness. Though they had only been partnered for a month, he had not seen this before.

"I will go easy when we figure out who is responsible for this crime," Saunders gritted out. "Ms. La Rue, I am going to have to ask you to stay here along with the others who were in the shop at the time. At least for the next few hours while we interview everybody."

Ms. La Rue, still looking quite pale at Saunders's demeanor, nodded hastily and went with a police officer ready to escort her to another area of the building.

Saunders dropped heavily to his chair, raking hands through his hair in palpable frustration.

Wickham mulled over his thoughts in the resulting silence. Why had Mr. Kennedy seemed so nervous at the questioning? Why had Ms. La Rue stated Mr. Smith's words as being different than Mr. Kennedy had? Why had both of them been found with stolen jewelry items in their pockets?

And how did Saunders know to write about diamonds and emeralds before Ms. La Rue spoke of them? He had known about Mr. Smith's identity, and he had become enraged when Ms. La Rue had nothing more to say, almost like Saunders knew that Mr. Smith *had* said something else.

A suspicion began to unfurl in the back of Wickham's mind. He did not want to indulge it, but could it be possible that Saunders was somehow aiding the criminal? He had knowledge that nobody else in the building—save Mr. Smith, to whom they had not yet spoken—should know. Still, it was possible that all of that was pure coincidence, and Wickham wanted to think that it was. He did not want to distrust his partner.

"Who else do we have to interview?" he asked, breaking the silence.

Saunders still seemed deep in thought, but he answered. "The manager, one Mr. Stanton, and two others who were in the store at the time, Miss Anderson and Mr. Hague. That makes up the five of them."

Miss Anderson, who was a brightly colored peacock of a woman, had been found with pearl earrings in her handbag. She insisted she did not know how they got there; she also agreed with Mr. Kennedy that the burglar had told them to lie on the floor.

On Mr. Hague's person had been discovered an emerald bracelet. He, too, said the burglar had said to lie on the floor, and Wickham made note of how suspiciously twitchy he seemed.

He and Saunders met at their desk once more before they went out to the crime scene.

The street outside Pendleton Jewelry teemed with curious people, all of them trying to peer past the police officers blocking their way. Wickham had to dodge as a horse plodded dangerously close to him, the irritated grumbling of the driver ringing in his ears.

"What happened?" one of the women in the crowd asked.

"I think someone got killed!" somebody answered.

"Killed? It was broad daylight. How does an honest, God-fearing man kill someone in broad daylight?"

A laugh sounded out, and the crowd jostled against one another. "Think it matters to them whether it's night or day?"

"Excuse me, ladies, gentlemen," Wickham said firmly, pushing a path through the crowd for him and Saunders. "We have a crime to solve and justice to uphold."

He heard a soft noise beside him; Saunders was laughing lowly. "That was dramatic."

Wickham gave his partner a confused look. "But we *are* here to uphold justice. We are detectives, Saunders. We stand alone in the face of—"

"Oh, God, spare me," Saunders groaned. "You have been a detective for just over a month and you think you are Sherlock Holmes. No, you think you are the *police* version of Sherlock Holmes, which I think may be even worse."

"I do not read fiction," Wickham sniffed. But he supposed Saunders was right, so he breathed out a sigh, bringing his chin down from where he'd been holding it quite high. He was only a junior detective, fresh out of the weeds.

Saunders clapped a hand to his shoulder. "There, there, Wickham. Plenty of time to learn, eh?"

The doorbell jingled merrily as they stepped into Pendleton Jewelry. It was just as nice inside as it was outside—the former was clad in white stone with sweeping arches, and the latter tastefully decorated, with dark wood and glass displays. A small cluster of police officers milled about the place, looking at damages.

"I just do not understand why someone would want to rob me in this day and age!" the manager was saying in distress. "It's 1921! You would think people these days would have a little more humanity."

"That is what we're here to find out, Mr. Stanton," Saunders said smoothly, shaking the manager's hand. A loud crash temporarily distracted Wickham; across the room, a young officer looked guilty at the broken windowpane he had broken even further.

Mr. Stanton repeated, in halting words, mostly the same story the others had given them. Where Mr. Kennedy had said the burglar had only stated his intention to rob the store, Mr. Stanton—like Ms. La Rue—said the burglar had specifically requested emeralds and diamonds.

Wickham looked at Saunders out of the corner of his eye. First the strange coincidence that Saunders knew things he perhaps should not, and then the fact that all of the customers had been found with stolen jewelry in their pockets. Wickham was beginning to get a headache. Could it be that the manager was the only innocent in this scenario?

It seemed ludicrous that the four customers and the criminal had somehow teamed up to rob the place. If Wickham added Saunders to that list, the prospect became even more ridiculous. They were all from very different walks of life, though the customers did share one thing in common. They were all rather rich.

"MR. SMITH is refusing to talk," Saunders told Wickham later in the evening as they sat at their desks. The light had grown dim, the office lit by a single bare bulb. Wickham's eyes were beginning to tire as he reread the official statements from all of them.

"Well, we'll just have to beat it out of him, won't we?" Wickham said valiantly.

Saunders gave him a strange look. "Are you *sure* you do not read detective novels? That is twice you have sounded like one today."

Wickham harrumphed and turned back to his paperwork. "We know that Mr. Smith is guilty. He was caught red-handed at the crime scene," he replied. "What I want to know is why La Rue, Kennedy, Hague, and Anderson all had stolen items too."

Saunders tiredly rubbed at his eyes. In the low light, his olive skin had taken on a pale hue, his dark eyes ringed with shadows. "I do not think we will be finding that out tonight. My vision is starting to swim. What say we pick this up tomorrow?"

It was a good idea. Wickham stood, covering a yawn with his hand. His elbow accidentally bumped against Saunders's side, and his apology almost drowned out the noise of a quiet jingle. "Oh? What have you got in there? I don't believe I've heard you jingle before," he teased.

Saunders laughed. "Just my keys, Wickham." He withdrew said keys from his pocket, the motion sending another item tumbling from his grasp. A necklace with emeralds and diamonds clattered to the desk.

"Saunders, you—"

"This is not what it looks like—"

Saunders did not get the chance to say anything more as Wickham manhandled him into a pair of handcuffs. "Help!" he cried. "I need assistance! I just caught Detective Saunders with stolen goods!"

Though Saunders wasn't struggling, two other policemen grabbed him and dragged him toward the door. "I swear, I did not steal it," Saunders shouted, eyes wide and desperate. "I did not know that it was in my pocket! Wickham, you have to believe me!"

The door slammed on his protests.


PENDLETON JEWELRY was back in business the next day.

Wickham watched people enter the store from his position across the street. It was raining, the droplets beating down hard on his fedora. A week ago, Saunders had amusedly told him he didn't *need* to stand in the rain when there was perfectly good shelter a few feet to his left.

Wickham scowled and moved. Once protected from the rain, he reached into his pocket to withdraw a battered packet of cigarettes, lit one, then inhaled deeply. He still could not believe Saunders was involved in the robbery. He had had suspicions after Saunders's strange knowledge, but he had not truly wanted to believe. Now it appeared Saunders would go the way of his previous partner—a compulsory discharge from the force. Perhaps even jail time.

The way things were going, everybody was guilty for this crime. Mr. Kennedy, Ms. La Rue, Miss. Anderson, Mr. Hague, Mr. Smith, and Saunders. Mr. Smith had been responsible for visibly robbing the place. The rest of them had been found with stolen jewelry. It could be some sort of minor crime ring. One of them had set it up and told the others of the profits they could gain, and the rest had fallen into place like greedy vultures.

A shout from across the road drew his eye, but it had not come from Pendleton Jewelry. A small group of men were exiting a small building, cursing amongst themselves about how the owner had refused to sell them alcohol. Wickham smiled. All along the street, multiple signs stated the same thing: *Closed for Violation of the National Prohibition Act*. People in this city had not taken kindly to the attempt to outlaw alcohol last year, and the police force's work had multiplied with the amount of illegal brewing going on.

The men who couldn't live without their alcohol just exasperated Weston. Although he had been one for the occasional drink, he was hardly suffering without it.

Still, a nice scotch might not go amiss right now. His head was beginning to hurt from the tangle of this case.

Wickham crossed the street and entered Pendleton Jewelry. He hung his coat and hat at the door, careful to make sure he didn't shake cast-off rain everywhere. "Detective," the manager, Mr. Stanton, greeted jovially. "Good afternoon to you. Al, this is one of the men who is trying to solve the case of who robbed my store!"

A worn cap made Al's expression inscrutable. The man stood at an average height, his sole distinguishing features a slight crooked tilt to his lips and a heavy brow. "Good old police, eh? Can always count on them to ruin the party." He spoke with a thick New York accent.

"My apologies, Detective. Al is not a friend of the law." Mr. Stanton laughed, clapping Al on the shoulder.

Were Saunders here, Wickham knew that he would be ruthlessly questioning Al already. Saunders was singular in the police force, with a zeal that was matched by no man. Wickham, however, just let it slide. Al, whatever he did, was not related to the case.

"Very few people are, these days," Wickham replied, nodding at Al.

"Those with throats as dry as dust, begging for a drop of alcohol to soothe it." Al smirked beneath his cap. "Are you a teetotaler, Detective?"

"I would be kicked out of my job if I was not. I must confess to a slight urge every now and again, but the solution is simple. Once men stop acting like rowdy dogs under the influence, I am sure the law will ease up on Prohibition," Wickham said.

Mr. Stanton mimed a toast. "And when that day comes, we will all have a drink to celebrate. Now, Detective, what brings you to my humble shop?"

"It is hardly humble," Al muttered.

"I came to follow up on the case," Wickham said.

"Ah," Mr. Stanton cried. "Have you found who did it?"

"Not yet, I am afraid." Wickham sighed. "Or, we have, but there are more suspects than we expected." He did not tell Mr. Stanton that his partner was one of them. Part of him still did not want to admit it out loud.

Mr. Stanton frowned. "More than you expected? How is that possible?"

"I cannot tell you too much," Wickham apologized. "I know you have already been interviewed by my colleagues, but I would like to run over the day with you again. There may be something we have missed."

"Very well," Mr. Stanton said. "As I told the police before, I was helping my customers. At the time that the burglar came into the store, I believe I was helping Ms. La Rue find a brooch. The burglar came in—he was wearing all black, with a mask that covered his face—and told us all to lie down on the floor because he was going to rob the place. We lay down, and while the burglar was in the back room, I rang the police. If I recall correctly, it took them ten minutes to arrive, and they caught the burglar just as he was exiting the shop."

It all sounded the same as what Wickham had heard before. "And Mr. Stanton, this may sound like an unusual question, but have you ever met Detective Saunders before?"

"Why, no, I do not believe I have," Mr. Stanton said thoughtfully. "Is that relevant?"

Wickham sighed. "No, Mr. Stanton. It was merely a question."

"Is Detective Saunders a suspect?" Mr. Stanton looked curious.

Wickham shook his head. He was not going to give away vital information to Mr. Stanton, even if the man had been robbed. That a detective was a suspect should be dealt with solely by the police for now.

"Well, I apologize for taking up your time, Mr. Stanton. Thank you for answering my questions."

"No, thank *you*, Detective, for working so vigilantly." Mr. Stanton shook Wickham's hand. As he withdrew his hand, it bumped up hard against Wickham's jacket, and Mr. Stanton laughed. "Apologies, Detective. My sight is getting poor in my old age."

"Good day, Mr. Stanton." Wickham nodded. "And to you, Al." He left the shop. Questioning the man had given him no new information.

The air grew chill as he made his way back toward the police station. The walk gave Wickham time to think and to reflect upon the case, to weigh up the testimonies in his mind. The case became more confusing by the minute, with too many suspects and none of them talking.

Before Wickham made the turn onto the street upon which the police office was housed, he reached into his pocket to find his cigarettes. Instead, his fingers closed on something cool and smooth.

It was a golden fob watch.

Startled, Wickham dropped it back into his pocket. He didn't own a golden fob watch. What was it doing in his pocket?

Like a flash, a memory caught his mind: Mr. Stanton shaking his hand and brushing against the side of his jacket.

Mr. Stanton had planted the watch on him!

Wickham ran back to the police station. He talked to the guard and had himself let in to the hallway of holding cells. The four customers sat at one end in a holding cell that looked more like a waiting room, and a smallish room with bars at the entrance held Saunders.

"Saunders," Wickham hissed, keeping his voice low.

Saunders did not appear to notice him at first. He sat on a wooden chair in the corner of the holding cell, his head hung low. Raising his head, he looked at Wickham, his expression none too happy. "Partner."

"Saunders, did you shake Mr. Stanton's hand when you met him?" Wickham leaned in closer to the bars.

"I did," Saunders said, his voice tight. "What of it?"

Wickham glanced around the hallway, making sure nobody was too close. "I believe Mr. Stanton planted that emerald and diamond bracelet on you."

Saunders rose. He looked tired, shadows lining his dark eyes. "Really? I thought you were too busy suspecting that your partner was involved in a jewelry heist."

Wickham frowned. "Oh, come now, Saunders. I go where the evidence points me, you know that."

Perhaps he should not have said that. Saunders took a step closer to the bars. "And what happened to trusting your partner above all else?" Saunders's face was like the expressive dark clouds that rolled in before a storm, his temper tightly leashed. For now. "What happened to those nights we spent up late, working on cases together? What happened to the times I covered for you when you were feeling ill? Did you decide to throw all of that away the second it was convenient?"

"Saunders." Wickham's voice had weakened. "I... I did not *want* to think you were guilty."

"Oh, then that makes it excusable," Saunders snapped. "You did not want to, but you did anyway."

Wickham took a deep breath, bracing himself. "I went to Pendleton Jewelry today," he said. "As I shook Mr. Stanton's hand, he brushed against my jacket. He said that his eyesight was just going, and apologized. But when I walked out, there was a golden fob watch in my pocket."

Saunders darted a glance down the hallway. "Have you shown anybody?"

"No."

"Good." Saunders glanced at Wickham's jacket. "Do *not* show anybody. They will think you a suspect too." After a second, his dark expression eased. "Dear God, Wickham. So you believe I am innocent now?"

"Yes, of course," Wickham replied. "I am sorry. My mind ran away with me, I am afraid." He reached through the bars to put a hand on Saunders's arm. "I *am* sorry, Saunders."

Saunders smiled. "You can make it up to me by proving my innocence, by proving that we are *all* innocent."

"I will get straight to it," Wickham promised. A long few seconds passed where he merely looked into Saunders's eyes. He withdrew his hand. "I should hopefully only be a few hours. I will get you out of here, partner."

FURTHER interviews got to the bottom of the story.

All four customers had shaken Mr. Stanton's hand as they'd entered Pendleton Jewelry. Mr. Kennedy's nervousness during the police interview, Wickham discovered, was due to a family history of criminal behavior, which Mr. Kennedy was thankfully not part of.

Ms. La Rue's memory issues turned out to be due to an illness. Because alcohol was prohibited, doctors now had to obtain special permits to prescribe alcohol for the use of health; Ms. La Rue currently took an ounce of alcohol every two hours for her anemia.

Miss. Anderson and Mr. Hague, too, were cleared of suspicion.

MR. SMITH was Wickham's last interview before he could present the case.

The man was in a more secure cell on the other end of the building, and he sat with his hands cuffed to the table. He was wan and gray-haired, perhaps fifty years at an estimate, and did not look to be the type of man to rob a jewelry store, now that Wickham saw him with his mask off.

"Mr. Smith," Wickham greeted him as he sat at the other end of the table. Now he just had to find out what role this man played in the crime. "My name is Detective Wickham. I am here to go over your statement again."

Mr. Smith gave a self-deprecating smile. "None of your colleagues believed me, Detective. Why would you?"

"I promise to be impartial."

"Very well. What do you want to hear?"

"Everything." Wickham pulled out his notepad. "But let us start with: what exactly was your aim in robbing Pendleton Jewelry?"

It might have seemed like a strange question. After all, the usual motivation for robbery was rather obvious. But because this was turning out to be such an unusual case, he thought he should ask.

"I was coerced," Mr. Smith said. "I was framed, Detective."

Wickham's eyebrows rose. "In what way?"

"You may recall that I was discharged from the police."

Wickham nodded. He did indeed.

"I am told there were a great many rumors surrounding that. The truth is, I suffered a bullet shot to the leg and was unable to recover fully from it. I was discharged and effectively retired. I took the job of a mechanic instead. My leg might be wounded, but my arms work just fine."

"And Detective Saunders was your previous partner, correct?"

"Correct." Mr. Smith smiled. "And now he is your partner. Are you two getting along?"

Wickham hurried the conversation along. "We will save that for another time, Mr. Smith. Now, you said you were coerced? By whom?"

"A week ago, Mr. Stanton came to me." Mr. Smith looked sorrowful. "He owns the building that I and my family live in. He said that unless I performed a job for him, he would kick us out. We are barely scraping along, Detective; we could not afford a move. If we tried, we would be destitute and end up living on the streets. I did not see that I had much option, and he told me nobody would get hurt."

"But why would Mr. Stanton want you to attempt to rob his store?"

"Insurance fraud. And the ability to sue." Mr. Smith smiled grimly. "But I was not the real patsy. I was just a diversion so that those four customers would walk out with 'stolen' jewelry in their pockets. Mr. Stanton said if I was charged—and I likely would not be, as he would not press charges against *me*, as I would not manage to actually steal anything—he would send money to my wife and children during my short stay in prison. Those four customers, however—they were rich. Rich enough that Mr. Stanton could get money out of them once they were found guilty."

That made no sense to Wickham whatsoever. Surely Mr. Stanton knew that, in the case of getting his stolen items back, he would be unable to sue. Was the man just uneducated about the ways of the law? Or did he have a deeper plan?

Wickham was beginning to get a headache. He pinched the bridge of his nose. He might as well indulge the line of thinking Mr. Stanton was following; otherwise, certain parts of this case would be too baffling to comprehend. "But why would Mr. Stanton need to do such a thing? He is already quite rich."

"I believe he has become involved in illegal alcohol production," Mr. Smith said. "Did you smell it at his shop?"

"Mr. Smith, are you aware of what you are saying?" Wickham stared at him. "Not only are you claiming that Mr. Stanton attempted to frame multiple people, but that he also has an illegal brewery at the back of his shop?"

"I am quite aware. I believe he wanted some extra money to kick off his side business, so to speak."

"And what happens when the police go to look for this brewery and find nothing?"

"Then I will be a liar, and you can put me behind bars." Mr. Smith looked firm in his resolve. "But I am not lying. I promise you that."

Wickham looked down at his notes. He had stopped writing halfway through the conversation, too stunned to keep noting down what he was hearing. But he believed Mr. Smith—there was no hint of a lie in the man's expression. Wickham was sure that if they hooked Mr. Smith up to one of those new lie detector machines, he would come out clean and free of deception.

But this case grew more and more confusing. Between Mr. Stanton thinking he could sue in the case of no financial loss—as the stolen items would be returned to him—and the arrogance of letting the police search a shop with a brewery in the back, Wickham's headache was just getting stronger. Mr. Stanton was either incredibly inept or thought entirely too much of himself.

"I will personally go investigate the whereabouts of this brewery," Wickham said. The sooner he found it, the sooner the innocent suspects could go free, including his partner.

"I heard that Detective Saunders is considered a suspect," Mr. Smith said. "I did not believe it as soon as I heard it."

"No?" The faith in Mr. Smith's eyes made Wickham feel somewhat guilty for thinking Saunders was involved.

"No." Mr. Smith laughed quietly. "I know you are new to working with him, so let me fill you in on a few things. Saunders believes in truth and the law above everything else. He is dedicated in a way that I have never seen in another officer. Sometimes it makes him seem self-righteous or too extreme."

Wickham thought back to the interview with Ms. La Rue, when Saunders had all but shouted at the woman because he believed she was holding something back. After Saunders had become a suspect, Wickham had assumed that episode was something more sinister.

"The truth is," Mr. Smith continued, "he just loves what he does."

"I see that now, Mr. Smith," Wickham replied softly. "And I owe him a personal apology."

"Just prove us all innocent, Detective. I think that would be apology enough."

Wickham left the cell and went back to his desk. He dropped his notepad on top of it, collapsing in his chair with a slow exhale. He would just give himself five minutes, and then he would return to Pendleton Jewelry.

His gaze caught on the various posters and portraits hanging on the wall to the side of his desk. They were familiar faces by now, long-wanted criminals every officer kept an eye out for. Wickham almost smiled as he looked at two of the oldest ones pinned side by side: an amateur cracksman and the strange, nervous-looking man who followed him around. Beside that was the infamous math professor, looking haughty even in the illustration.

The edge of a drawn heavy brow peeked out from behind a poster; Wickham leaned over to push the poster aside and was stunned by the face looking back at him. That brow, the slight crooked tilt to the lips, the worn cap…

It was Al, Mr. Stanton's friend.

His full name was Al Capone, and the poster said he was suspected of being involved with gangs and various illegal activities, such as the selling, consuming, and brewing of alcohol. That, Wickham reflected, must be why Al was at the jewelry store. He was aiding Mr. Stanton.

Wickham picked up his notepad again. It was time to go close this case.

THAT night, Wickham and Saunders stayed at the station later than usual, sitting on either side of Wickham's desk with a cup of coffee each. A small desk lamp provided the only light, dim yellow against white paper and dark wood.

"Did you see the look on Stanton's face when he was dragged away?" Saunders chuckled and took a sip of his coffee. "I imagine the bastard never thought he'd get caught. It's a good thing we have people like you working for us, Wickham."

Wickham laughed as well, but it was cut short by a sober expression. "I am sorry, Saunders," he said. "For doubting you."

"You go where the evidence leads." Saunders smiled, having clearly forgiven Wickham. "I was surprised by the jewelry in my pocket too. For a minute I even started to wonder if I had hit my head and stolen it in some strange mindless moment. It was protocol, Wickham. You were right to follow it."

"I still feel terrible," Wickham admitted. "But I assure you, from this moment on, I will trust you. I feel I understand you better now, Saunders. Your zeal for your work admittedly confused me at the start, but now I find it to be quite an admirable quality."

"As is your blockheadedness and tendency to overdramatize yourself," Saunders chipped in, and they laughed together.

Wickham settled back into his seat, feeling content. All was right with the world once again. He had his partner back, a man at his side whom he could trust above anybody else. The criminals were being charged and would be sent to prison, and life would carry on exactly as it should.

All in all, a good way to end the day.

---

# Chapter Seven

WESTON groaned pitifully against his pillow as the alarm shrieked at him. He'd finally been able to get some sleep after a big case, satisfied in his and Saunders's victory over the criminal manager of Pendleton Jewelry, and….

Weston opened his eyes, coming face to face with his alarm. His very modern, very digital alarm.

Weston leaped out of bed and nearly dropped his laptop twice in his haste to get it open. His fingers flew over the keys after he opened a new document, making spelling mistakes and grammar errors both in his fervor to write everything down before he forgot it.

It was *brilliant*. A regular 1920s detective novel, all laid out in his dream! It had everything: the brooding main character who relied on wits to solve the case, the sidekick, the mystery, the red herrings, the drama, the old-timey way of speaking.

Weston chose to ignore that the main character was more melodramatic than strictly brooding, and that some of the legal details about the case didn't quite add up. Of course they didn't—it was only a dream, and Weston could only write about the aspects of law that he knew about, which weren't very many, given that the majority of his knowledge came from court case television shows watched at five in the morning. He would simply have to research the rules of suing.

He was in the middle of describing Saunders when his fingers paused above his laptop keys. Saunders, with his olive skin and his brown eyes, his high cheekbones and dark hair, exactly matched the physical description of Sentry, the vilified dragon from his fantasy story. Who, in turn, looked like Sidney.

It had to be a coincidence. Plenty of men met that description.

Except what he'd been able to ignore while thinking about the fantasy setting now tickled at the back of his mind. He'd had two dreams like this—two unbelievably vivid dreams that contained whole stories, full of complex characters and settings Weston was simply unable to come up with in his waking thoughts. Twice now, the main character had been himself, in a strange, parallel universe kind of way. Twice now, those dreams had occurred after writing a small snippet of a story in the same setting.

And this was the second time there'd been a character who looked exactly like Sidney. Unfairly vilified, the victim of vicious rumor, and this time, Weston was sure that he—the main character—had felt something deeper for the Sidney character. It was all there in black and white, his notes glaring at him from his screen.

It was in the way Wickham and Saunders stared at each other for a little too long, in the end scene where they stayed together late at the office instead of heading their separate ways.

Weston snorted. Maybe this was just a sign that he needed to get laid.

He got up to make coffee, idly noting that it was a Saturday, thank God, and he didn't have anywhere to be. Weston divorced the characters of Wickham and Saunders from himself and Sidney in his thoughts. He picked through their personality and mannerisms as he put some bread in the toaster. That familiar thrum of inspiration was humming through him again, and it felt good.

Maybe *this* time he'd be able to write something. He hadn't had much luck with the high fantasy idea; perhaps he just didn't have the right kind of creativity to write high fantasy. Maybe a detective novel was more his style.

Over breakfast, Weston pondered the idea of doing a little detective work of his own. With Moran being fired yesterday, a lot of people had been wondering whether Sidney was really sick or just faking it so that he didn't have to face up to it. Some of the people around the office suspected Sidney was directly responsible for said firing. Before he really considered the legal ramifications of what he was doing, Weston sent an e-mail to Billy, the technician, asking for Sidney's address.

Two minutes later, Weston received a reply bearing Sidney's address. Billy had obviously decided to stretch his hacking skills.

Weston knew it was wrong. He absolutely knew that stalking the productivity consultant and confronting him at home would be wrong, but he was curious. He could frame it as professional concern.

He got dressed, shaved, and brushed, rehearsing what he'd say to Sidney when he discovered the man wasn't sick at all. Maybe he'd say, *You lying scumbag! You coward! You just can't face up to your own suggestions! I've caught you in the middle of your evil plan!*

No, that was a bit too melodramatic.

Perhaps: *Gee, Sidney, what a funny coincidence you happened to take a fake sick day after you suggested Moran be fired.*

No, that was too obvious. If only he could write his own dialogue like his subconscious did in his dreams.

On the drive to Sidney's address, Weston wound up pulling in at a diner. It was completely passive-aggressive, he knew, to order some chicken soup in a takeaway container. But the smug triumph of appearing concerned, only to be "disappointed" by a fake sickness, was too great to resist.

"I'm a terrible person," Weston said to himself in the car.

That didn't stop him from ringing Sidney's doorbell, though, chicken soup in hand. He ran over his potential script again, entirely ready to point his finger and shout something really damning.

A long half minute passed by. Weston started to wonder if Sidney was out. It was only ten in the morning on a *Saturday*, but maybe productivity consultants did crazy things like that.

The door creaked open, revealing Sidney.

Who looked *terrible*.

"You're sick," Weston said dumbly. "You look... really sick."

Sidney was pale, slouched in well-worn clothes. His hair was all over the place, and he was staring at Weston as though he didn't quite understand why he was there. "Weston?" he said. His voice was little more than a rasp.

"Uh." Weston blinked at him. At a loss for what to do, he shoved the container of chicken soup at Sidney. "Yeah. I heard you called in sick. I knew you were sick. Obviously."

Sidney peered down at the chicken soup. The little smile that spread over his lips made Weston feel even worse. "You brought me chicken soup," Sidney murmured. He took it slowly, as though even moving was difficult. "Thank you. That's really nice of you."

Sidney was Sentry was Saunders. It hit Weston in a flash, and he felt ridiculously stupid for not getting the hints his brain had been giving him. Sidney was suffering the same backlash of rumors and paranoid suspicion the two characters had been.

Freud and Jung would be so proud of him.

"Man, seriously, you look horrible," Weston said, concern creeping into his voice. "Do you need anything? Medicine or something? Would it be really weird if I just barged in right now and started fussing?"

"Probably." Sidney's smile had grown. "I should be quarantined for everybody's health."

That wasn't a no. And Sidney had moved aside, a subtle signal that Weston could come in if he wanted. So Weston did, taking the container from Sidney and pointing at the couch the man had obviously been lying on. "Couch. Go, now."

"Yes, sir." Sidney's voice held a quiet laugh as he shuffled back to the couch and sank on to it with a groan. The television was on, a trashy talk show playing. Out of the corner of his eye, Weston could see Sidney watching him, a faintly baffled expression on his face. He probably hadn't expected Weston to come in.

"Have you eaten?" Weston jiggled the container to draw attention to it, panicked at the thoughtless action, and remembered in relief that the soup was sealed in a plastic bowl.

Sidney stared blankly at him from the couch. "What time is it?"

"Just after ten."

"Ah." Sidney squinted in thought. After that contemplative hum of a noise, though, Sidney didn't say anything more.

Weston started to feel a bit paranoid. "What does that mean? Ah, I haven't eaten and I probably should? Or ah, I ate a frankly spectacular chicken soup two minutes ago, but I don't want to make Weston feel bad about his shitty diner chicken soup?"

Sidney's blank stare turned into an incredulous one. "The former, Weston."

"Okay." Weston inched sideways toward the kitchen. "Do you want shitty diner chicken soup?"

"I would love some." The softness in Sidney's voice helped ease Weston's jitters, at least.

"Where's your microwave?" Weston called, heading into the kitchen. It was an open area joined to the living room, which made Weston jealous. A guy could cook *and* watch television. That might make cooking so much less boring.

"On the right side. It's kind of hidden," Sidney replied.

Weston turned, frowned at the wood paneling covering everything, and then managed to unearth the microwave by sliding a panel upward. He set about heating the chicken soup, feeling a bit strange rattling about in Sidney's kitchen. But he was the one who had walked in, so he might as well follow through. Walking out would be even *more* awkward now.

Sidney had gone back to blankly staring at the television. He was wrapped in a thick blanket, a pile of tissues built up on the couch next to him. The sight made Weston smirk. Sidney was always so perfectly presented in the office; it was odd to see him so disheveled. It made him seem much more human, because Weston could relate. He'd gotten many a flu and spent entire days staring at crappy daytime television.

Armed with chicken soup in a bowl he'd found, a spoon, and a tea towel, Weston weaved around the kitchen counter. He laid the tea towel on Sidney's lap so that his legs didn't get too hot from the bowl, and sat the bowl on top of it, handing Sidney the spoon.

Sidney's baffled expression returned.

"I'm one of those people who can't bear to leave sick people alone," Weston offered as an explanation, smiling sheepishly. "Sorry. I get told it's annoying."

"No," Sidney said slowly, stirring the spoon around in the bowl. "It's... nice. It's really nice. Thank you, Weston."

Weston wasn't going to spend too long pondering the odd, happy warmth that settled in his gut at that. "Do you need anything else?"

Sidney shook his head, but he looked up at Weston. Pale and sleepy-eyed as he was, the hope on his face looked—dare Weston think it—pathetically adorable. "You could stay? I'm bored. Television is especially boring."

Weston hadn't expected that offer; it took him off guard, and he couldn't help but think about his intentions in coming here. He'd been so sure he was going to unearth devious motivations. Now he was playing nursemaid. "Sure," he said, settling onto the opposite end of the couch, careful not to disturb the tissue pile on the middle cushion. "I'm not super entertaining company, though, I'll warn you now."

"Oh, I'm sure that's not true." Sidney smiled as he blew on a spoonful of soup to cool it. "How is your tablet?"

Moment of truth. "It broke."

"It *broke*?" Sidney looked so distressed that he couldn't be faking it. Weston felt a little piece of his paranoia break off and turn into guilt. "That's terrible. What happened?"

"It was working fine before I went out to lunch," Weston sighed. "But when I came back, it wouldn't start up. I looked through the manual and tried resetting it and everything. I even took it to one of our technicians, but he said I should send it back."

"I'm sorry, Weston." Sidney looked upset. "Do you think it's because I changed the order to a newer model?"

The part of Weston still stuck in paranoia mode, the lingering irritation over his tablet breaking, wanted to answer, *Yes, it was your fault; you should let me get the one I chose.*

"No." In the end, thinking that was just irrational. "No, it's just one of those rare things that happens, I guess. Even brand-new models ship out with occasional faults. It's not your fault." Weston gave Sidney a little smile. "Besides, I started to really like the tablet."

"Did you?" Sidney was obviously relieved by that. The expression looked good on him, the smile curling at the edge of his lips, his dark eyes alight. "I'm glad. I have a few artist friends who swear by them."

"Yeah, it took a while to get used to," Weston replied with a nod. He started to relax into the easy conversation now and leaned back against the couch. "I'm so used to scratching pencil against paper that the tablet surface was a bit weird at first. But it was pretty easy to use once I got used to it."

Sidney made a pleased noise as he tasted the soup. "Are you going to get one for use at home now? I'm sure Sanderson can get you a deal."

"Oh, I don't… draw at home," Weston said awkwardly.

"Why not?" Instead of the disbelieving scoff Weston expected, Sidney just looked curious. "I've seen your work. You're very good. You've got a real eye for detail."

Weston fell silent with a vague shrug. He turned his gaze back to the television, where a woman was showing off her botoxed-permanently-into-surprise eyebrows and fighting with another woman wearing an eye-rending glittery golden dress. The line at the bottom of the screen read: *I Am the Reincarnation of Cleopatra. So Am I!*

"I used to," Weston eventually offered. "I just sort of stopped. It's stupid, really."

Sidney poked him with the spoon. "Do tell."

Weston gave him a mock-disgusted look. "Did you just poke me with your gross spit-covered spoon?"

"I did." Sidney's smile was positively wicked. "And I'll do it again, if you don't share."

"Ugh. Fine." Weston gave an exaggerated shudder. "Anything to avoid *cooties*."

Sidney's peal of laughter, though slightly hoarse, was something Weston found himself enjoying the sound of.

"Well, I drew a lot when I was younger. Way back in school. I started when I was thirteen or so. I was addicted to it, I drew all over everything. My schoolbooks, my notepads, random scraps of paper. When I didn't have anything else to draw on, I drew on my arms with felt-tips. I used to think it looked cool, like a sleeve tattoo."

He huffed a laugh at the memory of it. "I was so *passionate* about art back then. My parents and my friends always used to tell me I was so good, that I was destined to be an amazing artist— because I was a kid, you know? Nobody criticizes the art of kids. So I thought I was a great artist and that everything I drew was awesome. I enjoyed every single minute of it, because I produced art that I loved looking at afterward. I didn't know what cliché was, and I didn't care, because I had so many ideas that I thought were so original, so unique."

On the television, the two women had started engaging in a slap fight, which was temporarily distracting. Weston smirked and returned to talking; Sidney was listening attentively, curiosity still in his expression. "Anyway, so I got older. I applied to an art college and got in. I was still convinced that I was an amazing artist, that everybody would be in awe of my skill. Full of the arrogance of youth, I guess. I sat down in my first class, and we passed our notebooks around. And I realized something, looking at the art of everyone around me: I was *average*. Not even average. I was so thoroughly *below* average that it was a little soul crushing."

What he was not going to tell Sidney was that he'd cried once he'd gotten back to his dorm room. That was too embarrassing to share.

"And suddenly, everything I started to draw sucked. All of my ideas had been done before by better artists than me. I could see all the mistakes in the finished product; I couldn't stop comparing myself to better artists. And all of that excitement I used to draw with, it was gone, because I didn't love what I drew anymore." Weston gave a sigh and a rueful smile. "It's pretty childish, in hindsight. I finished that degree, but I didn't draw for fun outside of college work. I just never managed to work up that passion again."

Sidney, at least, looked understanding. When Weston had told Henry why he'd stopped drawing, Henry had laughed and told him to grow up and get over it. Which was valid, Weston supposed.

"You write now, don't you?" Sidney asked.

"Yeah." Weston shrugged. "That's the funny difference between writers and artists. When writers read a great book, they get inspired. When artists see a great painting, they get jealous and despair that they'll never be that good. It's probably why you hear of so many crazy-as-shit artists—they're all fucked in the head."

"*You're* all fucked in the head," Sidney corrected gently.

Weston frowned at him. "What?"

"You're still an artist, Weston," Sidney said. "When I look at your designs, I can see some of your passion for it is still there. You just need to find it again."

Weston snorted, but he didn't reply. He didn't agree, but since Sidney was sick, Weston would give him a break and not turn the conversation into a treatise on how much he sucked at art.

"Do you think you'll ever draw for fun again?" Sidney had nearly finished his soup; he must have been hungry to eat it that quickly.

"I hope so," Weston murmured. "Every once in a while I try again. But it's a stupid vicious circle. I don't practice because I think I'm bad. And I'm bad because I don't practice."

Sidney's laugh was soft. "I'm sure you'll get that passion back one day, Weston. I said I was friends with a few artists, remember? I've seen their cycles. They worry themselves sick and cover their paintings with black paint because they think it's so hideous it should never see the light of day, but then they work at it and they gain some confidence back. At least none of them have cut off an ear yet."

Weston had to laugh as well. "Van Gogh joke. Nice."

"A friend is obsessed," Sidney replied. "If she could, I think she would plaster *The Starry Night* upon every single one of her apartment walls."

Weston gave a teasing scoff. "That's so mainstream. Tell her to like something else, like *Prisoners Exercising*."

"I'll be sure to tell her that." Sidney smirked, leaning forward to set the bowl on the coffee table. He leaned back with a groan, curling the blanket tighter around himself with a shiver.

"Are you okay?" Weston half leaned over in concern. He'd been so distracted by Sidney's expressions that he'd all but forgotten the man was sick.

Sidney waved a blanket-covered hand. "I'm fine. Just the typical flu symptoms, achy and everything. I think the bug's going around."

"Yeah, one of the women at work has a kid with it." Weston wondered if Judy was doing okay. He hoped so—young children tended to get hit hard when they got the flu. "Do you know Judy?"

"I haven't had the opportunity to talk to her yet, but yes, I know who she is," Sidney said. "Her productivity is through the roof. She's an excellent worker." He paused, an embarrassed look creeping onto his face. "Don't tell anybody I said that. I probably shouldn't be sharing those reports with you."

"Oh, do tell," Weston parroted Sidney's earlier words. "What's my report like? Is it terrible?"

"I'm not telling you," Sidney sighed, giving a mock roll of his eyes.

"Not even if I get you really, really drunk?"

"Not even if you get me really, really drunk." Sidney looked solemn, but there was a mischievous smile in his eyes. "Not even on rum."

"So you're saying you have a low tolerance for rum," Weston mused, raising his eyebrows. "Thank you. That's very useful information."

Sidney groaned. "Damn it, I've given away my weakness."

Laughing to himself, Weston settled back against the cushions. The twin Cleopatras and their slap fight had resulted in a clear winner; the one with surprised eyebrows was smirking in the camera, declaring herself victorious. "Thank you," Weston wound up saying. "For not laughing at my stupid art story."

"Why would I laugh?" Sidney looked puzzled.

"It's just stupid and childish, I guess." Weston picked at a stray thread on his jeans. "I've been told I should get over it and realize that everybody thinks they suck."

"Well, yes, most people do think they're bad at their various creative endeavors," Sidney replied, turning his head to look at Weston. "But passion for it is found and broken in a lot of different ways, and none of them are stupid."

"That was poetic," Weston said dryly. He appreciated the sentiment, though. Maybe he'd even believe it one day.

As Sidney gave a hum of agreement, they fell into a comfortable quiet. It reminded Weston of their lunch at the café—he hadn't expected to be able to have nonawkward silences with Sidney, but there it was, happening. The apartment was lit only by a few lamps, the television providing most of the illumination. Sidney sniffled every once in a while, his breathing thick, and he occasionally grunted quietly as he shifted to get more comfortable.

It *should* have been irritating. As much as he fussed over sick people, Weston didn't particularly enjoy their company. There were germs, and snot, and all kinds of gross sick things. The sounds they made were disgusting. It wasn't the best way to get to know a person. But he just leaned forward, grabbed the tissue box off the coffee table, and handed it to Sidney. Questions about what Sidney was doing at their work still floated around in the back of Weston's mind, but they didn't seem so immediate now.

Perhaps it was silly to start to trust Sidney based on two— albeit incredibly vivid—dreams. But whenever Weston looked at the man now, he couldn't help but see shades of those characters in his face, the strength of Sentry in his eyes, the resolve of Saunders in the line of his jaw.

God. His brain was getting carried away.

When the television show ended and the Cleopatras bid regal farewells to the viewers, Weston asked, "Do you need anything?"

Sidney rolled his head on the back of his couch to look at Weston. "Are you going to ask that every half hour now?"

"Yes," Weston said stubbornly. "It gets upgraded to every fifteen minutes if you start coughing."

Sidney chuckled lowly. "Then no, I'm all right at the moment. I feel a bit better, actually. I think being entertained is doing me some good."

"Good." Strangely, Weston was quite content to just sit around and do nothing. He had nothing to do for the day, and he didn't feel the need to try to get started writing that detective story idea just yet.

When the next horrible daytime talk show was well underway, Weston got up to get a glass of water. He noticed Sidney's eyes were closed, and he paused in his walk, staring. Had Sidney fallen asleep? Weston knew sleeping would be good for him right now, but it was also pretty awkward. What was he supposed to do if Sidney decided to sleep for the rest of the day? If he just hung around his apartment, that might be more than a little creepy.

He settled on gently prodding Sidney's shoulder. "Hey," Weston said lowly. "Don't fall asleep on the couch. A bed would be way more comfortable."

A traitorous part of his brain snickered.

Weston mentally rolled his eyes at himself. Just because Sidney was reasonably attractive didn't mean that immature giggling about beds was appropriate. He hated his brain sometimes.

"Hmm?" Sidney blinked groggily. "Oh God, I'm sorry, Weston. I didn't mean to drift off." He looked like a burrito in his swath of blankets, and he struggled to move, trapped in them and clumsy.

"It's okay." Weston laughed. "I just didn't want you to wake up with a crick in your neck."

He also didn't want to be a creepy stalker who hung around while people napped.

"Bed, yes," Sidney said, managing to stand up. The hair at the back of his head was sticking straight out, and Weston only barely managed to quash a laugh at the sight of it. "Bed is good."

"Bed *is* good," Weston agreed, having progressed to smirking. "Go get some sleep, Sidney. I'll let myself out."

Obviously still half-asleep, Sidney shuffled down the hallway, the blanket occasionally tripping him up. "Night, Weston," he called around a yawn.

It wasn't nighttime, but Weston didn't correct him. "Get better soon," he replied, watching for a moment longer just to make sure Sidney didn't stumble, fall, and break his head open. Once he appeared to make it safely to the bedroom, Weston let himself out.

The bright sunlight hurt his eyes after so long in the darkened room, making him squint as he walked to his car.

He felt good—mellow and relaxed—because of *Sidney*. That was just strange, but Weston figured he might as well embrace it. He hadn't addressed the question of whether or not Sidney had made the suggestion to fire Moran, but all of a sudden it didn't seem to bother him much. Sure, Moran was out of a job, but Sidney was just so surprisingly *likable*.

That was probably a terrible thing for him to think. Poor Moran.

By Monday, Sidney was back at work.

Weston only caught a glimpse of him through the glass wall of his office before Sidney moved out of sight, so he couldn't tell if Sidney still looked sick. He'd spent the Sunday running errands and attempting to write a bit; the latter activity hadn't produced any fruitful results, much to Weston's frustration. The main character, Wickham, kept talking about horrible stereotypes and refused to part with his fedora.

Weston knew he controlled the characters, of course he did. But they also seemed to have lives of their own when he attempted to write them. He'd read once that Arthur Conan Doyle had a love-hate relationship with Sherlock Holmes as a character because the character kept trying to do things Doyle didn't intend for him to do. Weston could relate. Then again, Arthur Conan Doyle also hated Holmes for becoming incredibly popular and eclipsing his other works. Weston sadly could not relate to that.

He'd picked up pencil and paper supplies while his tablet was being fixed, and had to work through the frustration of going back to it after he'd started to like the tablet. On one hand, it was like going back to a beloved childhood home. On the other, he'd just discovered that said beloved childhood home had terrible plumbing and a rat infestation. Eraser rubbings were getting everywhere.

His workmates had been surprisingly quiet. Henry hadn't even come in for his morning Let's Bother Weston routine, which Weston found strange; he enjoyed Henry's company, and it was odd to start a day without it. However, when he'd gone to get coffee, he had seen Henry around the corner, head down and working hard. Aiko had been much the same.

Perhaps they had been scared into working harder by Moran being fired. Weston supposed that was a good thing; more productivity could never be bad.

Halfway through the morning, Aiko knocked on his door.

"We've got your latest design made up," she informed him.

"You look rather professional today," Weston noted in greeting.

She gave him a withering stare. "Do you want to see it or not?"

Women. Weston didn't understand them. Hadn't he just paid her a compliment? Or had she taken that as a subtle jab at her *not* usually looking professional?

"Sure, yeah. Is it here?" Weston stood. "Mr. Kent's coming around in half an hour; it'd be great to show him the prototype."

The prototype, it turned out, was hideous. Weston had designed it—he knew how it looked on paper, and he'd hated every minute of it. But the sewers had done a damn good job on it, considering the complicated design.

After hauling the suit out of the plastic bag it had come wrapped in, Weston draped it over a mannequin bust in his office. There it was, in all its red puffer fish-squirrel glory. Aiko was laughing, and Weston couldn't find it within himself to blame her.

"*You* designed that?" she said.

"Yes," Weston replied miserably. "It's what the guy wanted. It's a sports team mascot, and it's been around for years. I couldn't change it."

Aiko reached out to poke one of the soft spikes that protruded from all over the suit. "It's hideous." She smirked. "I almost want to give you an award. Designer of the World's Worst Mascot Suit."

"Thanks," Weston said dryly. "But actually, genuine thanks for bringing this to me—I'd completely lost track of time."

"No problem." She waved a hand at him, bright-red nail polish catching the office lights. "Lunch later?"

"Sure." As Aiko left, Weston examined the suit, heaving a sigh and returning to his desk. The fluffy squirrel tail was constantly in the corner of his vision.

Mr. Kent, when he turned up half an hour later, loved it. And Weston was doomed to watch as an associate Mr. Kent had brought along tried the suit on. Just to get the damn thing out of his office, Weston encouraged that they take a walk around the building to see if it held up to movement.

As Weston watched them move slowly down the hallway, Henry came to stand next to him.

"How do people *like* the shit I give them?" Weston despaired.

"You have a gift," Henry said.

The associate pulled a string under the suit's arm, and the whole thing puffed up with a cheerful hiss, bloating out to resemble a puffer fish.

"A terrible, *terrible* gift," Henry amended.

They stared until Mr. Kent and his associate finally disappeared from view. "He'll be back," Weston groaned, scrubbing his hands through his hair. "And I'll have to look at it again. You have to save me, Henry."

"Sorry, you're on your own." Henry snorted. "We're having lunch later, right?"

"Yeah, I already confirmed with Aiko. Didn't she tell you?"

"I wanted to make sure."

Weston frowned. "You have that look on your face like you're plotting something. What are you plotting?"

He had to think about it for a moment to make sure, but no, it wasn't April Fools' Day. Nor was it his birthday or any other special day that might require Henry getting that little smirk at the corner of his mouth.

"Nothing." Henry looked the very picture of innocence—or at least attempted to. "Nothing at all. Just meet us outside at twelve thirty."

When Mr. Kent came back, Weston felt a little better after the praise the man heaped on him. According to Mr. Kent, his work was *revolutionary* and *genius*, and he would be known for years to come as a visionary artist. Weston doubted that, considering his achievement was a red puffer fish-squirrel abomination that inflated, but he happily took the praise nonetheless, shaking Mr. Kent's hand and telling him he was welcome to come back at any time.

With his mood lifted, Weston happily delved into the next of his projects—this one a rather more sane design of a blue jay. He saw Sidney pass his office once or twice more, but he seemed busy, so Weston didn't interrupt him.

His thoughts kept going back to Saturday, though. He'd seen an entirely human side of Sidney that was, admittedly, oddly appealing. Gone had been the slightly cold, efficient demeanor of the person Weston saw at work. He'd seen none of the strangeness or the overly reserved man office rumor painted Sidney to be.

Lunchtime rolled around. Weston left his designs scattered haphazardly across his desk, eager to get out for some fresh air. Expecting the usual crowd, he was surprised when he saw Sidney standing just outside the door.

"Good afternoon," Sidney said, looking happy to see him.

"Hey, how are you feeling?" Weston, personally, was experiencing none of the awkwardness that had previously characterized his interactions with Sidney.

"Much better." Sidney *looked* better too, Weston noted. His skin was no longer the pale pallor of sickness, and his eyes were nearly free of the shadows underneath them. Though Sidney still looked tired, he looked to be on the way to recovery. "It was just one of those short flu bugs, looks like."

"Good." Weston smiled at Sidney. "You didn't get too brain-dead from all that daytime television?"

Sidney grinned in reply. "Nearly. And thank you again for Saturday; the chicken soup was much appreciated."

Weston had expected that Sidney might feel a bit strange around him. After all, Weston was only a coworker, one who had barged into Sidney's house to fuss over him after being rather suspicious of him for some time. Thankfully, the conversation seemed to be going easily enough.

"Well, I'm glad it helped. I—"

Henry, Aiko, and Judy all walked out as a crowd; Henry was laughing loudly enough that it interrupted Weston. "There you are," he said cheerfully, wrapping an arm around Weston's shoulders. "We ready?"

Weston glanced at Sidney. Suddenly he felt bad about not inviting the guy to lunch, but seeing as Henry and Aiko didn't like him, inviting him along with them would just turn lunch into a horrendously awkward affair.

"We're ready," Sidney confirmed.

Weston nearly did a double take. They'd invited Sidney?

Apparently so, because Sidney started walking side-by-side with them as they headed down the street. Henry and Aiko rather obviously stayed at a distance from him, putting Judy and Weston between them and Sidney, but no barbs or curses were flying. Weston wondered if this was their attempt to apologize to Sidney for perpetuating cruel rumors about him.

The idea made Weston smile, and he passed the time during their walk with small talk. The weather wasn't the most interesting topic of conversation, but it was meaningless enough, and a safer topic than work. Sidney wasn't smiling as openly now, but Weston caught him darting little glances toward the rest of them, his eyebrows raised in what looked like hope.

Sidney was *shy*, Weston realized. He felt like an idiot for not realizing it sooner. It explained some things: the stiff demeanor toward people at work, the quiet way he kept to himself and didn't socialize much. It wasn't that he was cold or standoffish, he was just nervous about interaction.

"Huh," Weston said out loud.

Only Sidney heard him, but at Sidney's querying look, Weston just shook his head. "Nothing, just thinking out loud."

They piled into their usual café, Sidney taking up a seat opposite Weston and next to Judy. Though he went there several times a week, Weston still looked up at the menu board to read it.

"So, guys," Aiko announced, lifting her briefcase onto her lap. "You might be noticing that we have an extra lunch-goer along with us today." When Weston grinned at Sidney, pleased at his presence—and definitely pleased that Henry and Aiko had invited him—Sidney's smile was small, polite, but perfunctory to the casual viewer.

Huh. He really *was* shy.

"I have a present for you, Sidney," Aiko continued. She held up a shiny red travel mug, complete with a bow around the top, and leaned over the table to present it to Sidney. "Careful, it's hot." She grinned. "I prefilled it. But I saw that you don't have an office mug like everybody else does, so I thought I might get you one."

Sidney carefully took the mug, his eyes widening. "Wow, thank you for this." A pleased expression started to creep over his features.

"Huh, I knew she was getting you a present, but I didn't know what," Henry remarked. He looked jealous. "Why didn't you get *me* one of those?"

"Because you're not new." Aiko rolled her eyes.

"I'm not even going to ask how you knew what color I liked," Sidney said, smiling.

Aiko waved a hand. "Call it women's intuition. And you're welcome. I just thought I should properly welcome you to the office, Sanderson Designs style."

After turning the mug around in his hands a bit, Sidney raised it to his lips to take a sip. The mug had obviously only been filled halfway, and when Sidney raised it enough, Weston could see words printed on the bottom of the mug. It read:

*I'M AN ASSHOLE.*

A sick feeling clutched at the back of Weston's throat, a coldness settling into his gut. Aiko was smirking to herself, and Henry had started laughing uproariously.

"What?" The smile still caught at the edge of his lips, Sidney looked at them, clearly expecting them to let him in on the joke. "What's so funny?"

Weston opened his mouth to reply but found he couldn't. Judy did so for him. "Never mind them, Sidney," she muttered, shooting venomous looks at Henry and Aiko. "It's not funny at all."

Sidney was still curious, though, and he'd obviously figured out that something was on the bottom of the mug. He lifted it up to take a look. His smile froze.

"Guys, come on," Weston said uselessly. He couldn't figure out what mix of emotions he felt: anger, upset, guilt, even though he'd had nothing to do with this. "That's a dick move. They don't mean it, Sidney."

All of the pleasantly surprised expression had gone from Sidney's face, replaced with a clenched jaw. "Of course. I can take a joke," he said evenly.

"Of course he can," Henry agreed happily, slapping Sidney on the shoulder.

In what had to be the fakest move that Weston had ever seen, Sidney "found" a text message on his phone. "Oh, I'm terribly sorry, but I have to go," he said. His voice was still flat. Weston wasn't sure if he was genuinely attempting to make them think he actually had to go or if he knew full well nobody had believed his little pantomime and kept up the charade to rub his deliberate leaving in their faces. "Thank you for the offer of lunch. And the mug. I'll see you back at the office."

He left. Weston wasn't thinking as he shoved back his chair and rushed to follow.

"Sidney!" he said, taking two quick steps to catch up, narrowly dodging passers-by as they got out onto the street. "Shit, I'm so sorry. I didn't know they were going to do that."

Sidney's eyes narrowed. "Didn't you?"

"No!" Weston gaped at him. "Jesus, I might be fucked in the head, but I'm not *cruel*. And that was cruel."

He still felt guilty by association. Henry and Aiko were his friends, and what was more, he'd previously been just as suspicious and hateful as they had been.

Sidney peered at him for a few more seconds before he sighed, the tense lines in his face easing slightly. "No, I didn't think you were a part of that," he said, sounding relieved but still unhappy. "Don't worry about it, Weston. I suppose I should have expected it, given how wary people are of me at the office."

Right. Sidney the productivity consultant.

Weston was surprised to not feel any ire toward that anymore. Well, maybe a little. But just a little.

"They think you suggested that Moran should be fired," he explained, having to dodge a man who gave him a venomous glare for stopping in the middle of the sidewalk. Wincing, Weston took a step to stand closer to a shop window, getting out of the way of people walking.

"I did," Sidney said.

Weston blinked at him. "Oh. Well, that's why they're angry." He felt some of that old paranoia returning.

"Weston, the last thing I want to do is put people out of their jobs," Sidney sighed. "But to be blunt, Moran wasn't good for the company. And I'm sure you'd realize that, if you think about his habits and productivity."

"I didn't really know the guy that well," Weston pointed out nervously.

"You probably knew he was a drinker," Sidney said. "If you'd ask Judy, she'd tell you Moran came in to work every morning hungover. Sometimes still drunk. His work rate was frankly atrocious, and the number of errors he made on a daily basis was shocking. I don't mean to sound harsh, but Sanderson hired me to make sure his company was earning the best profit it could. Workers that barely work aren't good for profit."

Weston had to admit Sidney had a point, now that he thought about it. Moran had been friendly and loud, but everybody in the office knew he had to be an alcoholic. Judy had—she'd told him, even gone to Sanderson several times—but Moran had kept his job.

"Shit." Weston rubbed a hand over his forehead. He'd gotten so caught up in everything that he'd failed to remember that. All he'd been able to think about was a fellow worker losing his job. "You're right. Of course you're right, that's your job, and I'm sure you're good at it."

Sidney smiled, but the expression still bore a trace of hurt. "I like to think I do okay."

"Look, I'm sorry about the mug. If I'd known Aiko was going to do that, I would have stopped her." Weston grimaced. "I think Henry knew something like that was going to happen. He's not normally like that." He couldn't believe Henry would advocate something that cruel. The man did tend to sling friendly insults at his friends, but he wasn't socially inept—he knew the difference between doing that with friends and doing it with people he barely knew.

"It's not your fault." Sidney was still grasping the mug.

"You can throw that away if you want," Weston pointed out. "I recognize the brand; it's just two-dollar-store crap."

Sidney laughed, near silently. "I'm not going to throw it out. I can still use it. Just not around people, I suppose."

Weston had to admire the man's stubbornness. Were that him, he would have thrown it in the nearest trash can by now. He was beginning to suspect that Sidney was made of much sterner stuff than him. "Yeah? At least you'll never see the bottom of it when you're drinking it."

"Exactly." Sidney gave him a smile. It was still wan, and the smile barely crinkled the corner of his eyes, but it was there. "Maybe one day I'll even get a laugh out of it."

"Let's go to lunch somewhere else," Weston offered on a whim. "Fuck Henry and Aiko. We can find a better café." When Sidney paused more than a few seconds to reply, Weston added, "It's on me."

"Well, I can hardly refuse free lunch," Sidney said. The smile didn't grow, but it didn't dim either, so Weston counted that as a victory.

"Come on, I know a good place." Weston turned in the other direction and led them down a narrow side street that emerged onto another busy pathway. The streets here were always crowded during lunchtime, and Weston still hadn't figured out the fine art of people-dodging. But he managed to get them to a little café tucked away between two department stores. The outside was plastered with concert posters decorating every inch of wall space, and the inside was much the same.

Number 4, the café was called. Weston had no idea of the origin of the name, and it was a place he came to rarely—Henry didn't like it, for reasons Weston couldn't comprehend. It was tiny and packed with people, small tables lining one wall, and a big wooden communal table in the center.

Weston found the one table in the café that wasn't occupied, and squeezed into the narrow fit. When Sidney sat, their knees knocked together underneath the table. "Sorry." Weston laughed, trying to shift to give Sidney more leg room. "It's kind of cramped."

"No, I like it." Sidney looked around in fascination at the interior decorating. His eye seemed to catch on a huge ceramic lion sitting on a ledge near the ceiling, and he smirked a little. "The little pool balls in their individual cages are an interesting touch. I like the inflatable penguin in the corner too."

"Cafés with character are the best kind of cafés," Weston agreed. "The food here is really good too. I promise you'll like it."

He started to get déjà vu as they studied their menus together. Only this time he felt as though he knew Sidney a lot better—that, and he'd stopped harboring suspicions that Sidney was secretly out to destroy the business. What had seemed like such valid reasons before now seemed silly and embarrassing. Weston knew he worked hard, and he was sure his productivity reports were fine.

After they'd ordered, Weston amused himself by looking over the various decorations. They were part of why he liked the café so much, and Sidney seemed entranced by them as well. Weston tried not to stare too much; he wanted to try to cheer Sidney up. Though he wasn't great at doing that for people, he wanted to try, seeing as it was his friends who had upset Sidney. It wasn't easy to see, looking at the man. He carried his expressions in bare quirks at the corner of his lips most of the time, in the faint frown lines at the edge of his eyes.

Which was why it was so satisfying to point out a tacky camel lamp in the corner of the café and see Sidney grin, free and unreserved.

"Double espresso?" Their waiter had returned, questioning eyes under a shock of blue hair.

"That's me, thank you," Sidney said, accepting the coffee.

The waiter's eyes lingered on Sidney. "Your food will be out in just a minute."

"Oh, thank you." Sidney's tone tipped upward at the end, slightly confused.

Weston was confused too. The waiter had now progressed into loitering, standing at the edge of their table, clearly trying to come up with something to say. "Right," he said, then paused. "I'll be back with your food later."

As he left, Sidney smiled in bemusement, sharing a look with Weston. Then Weston realized what had been happening—the waiter had been *flirting*.

Weston really shouldn't feel a pang of jealousy over that.

But come to think of it, he didn't even know if Sidney was gay. The odds were not in his favor. Not that he was thinking about Sidney's sexuality and wondering if he'd be receptive to flirting. Not at all.

"Are you gay?" Weston blurted. And then mentally kicked himself.

Why was he so awkward?

Sidney's eyebrows rose. He looked startled at first, and then the bemusement came back. "Are you wondering if I'll vanish into the bathroom with the waiter? Don't worry, I won't leave you stranded."

That hadn't actually answered his question, but since Weston wasn't sure if he should ask it again, he gave a little laugh in lieu of a reply. It was easier than thinking of how to apologize for being such a spaz.

"I hear you are," Sidney said. "Gay, I mean."

"*What*?" Weston didn't shriek. Really. It was an entirely masculine bellow of surprise. "Who told you? Do you have *really* good gaydar?"

"My God, Judy's right. You do flail." Sidney peered at Weston in interest, head cocked.

"It was Judy." Weston groaned. "She told you."

Sidney laughed quietly. "I'm sorry. I didn't ask, if that's what you're thinking. I was talking to her, and the topic turned to you. She mentioned that you needed to find yourself, and I quote, 'a nice, calm man'."

Mollified, Weston shrank down in his seat. He was going to have to give Judy a stern talking to. Still, he wasn't exactly in the closet, so it didn't really bother him who knew. It was just a surprise. "Yeah, well, I have other things to focus on," he muttered. "Like driving every potential partner away with my hysterics and horrible habits."

"I'm sure you're not *that* bad," Sidney assured him, still amused. "But for your curiosity, yes, I am gay."

Weston cursed his traitorous heart for skipping a beat. This was getting ridiculous. He was not interested in Sidney. "Oh. Okay," Weston replied. "Yay?" He mimed waving a pride flag, a little back and forth of a held-up hand.

Sidney stared at him. "I'm beginning to think you're more awkward at conversations than I am. And one of my long-running nicknames is the Ice Queen."

Weston felt his cheeks go a little red, but Sidney was smiling at him, taking the sting out of his words. "Blame an overactive imagination generally being more interesting than most people."

"I'll take that as a compliment, seeing as I've yet to see you space out on me," Sidney said.

That was true, at least. But Weston declined to mention that Sidney had featured twice in extremely vivid, complicated dreams that he hoped to use as inspiration for future writing. He had a feeling bringing *that* up might be somewhat awkward.

The waiter came back and took a little too long setting their plates down in front of them. He was sneaking furtive glances at Sidney, and Weston tried not to scowl. He had no right to be jealous; he had no claim on Sidney whatsoever. Instead, he distracted himself with how good his tortellini smelled, and eagerly dug in. Thank God for long lunch breaks.

They lapsed into comfortable silence again, sharing amused glances when pop songs started playing through the speakers, occasionally trading remarks about what songs they liked and which they didn't. Weston discovered Sidney was an old-school rock kind of man, which pleased him to no end, though they couldn't decide who was better, Eric Clapton or Led Zeppelin. Weston tried to argue that they weren't comparable, which turned the conversation on to the topic of Morris Day and The Time, which they both agreed was definitely not comparable to anything else. Weston swore by "Jungle Love" as one of the greatest songs to drive to.

It was starting to get difficult, avoiding that warmth in his chest every time he got Sidney to laugh or grin. Each time, Weston just shoved it down. He was sure he and Sidney were ill matched, and he was not the type of man to entertain stupid fluttery feelings for somebody he barely knew, let alone a colleague.

THE minute Weston got back to work, Aiko was in his office, giving him a suspicious glower.

"What the hell was that at lunch?" she asked.

"That was me not finding your gift very funny," Weston muttered, keeping his head down as he looked through his desk drawers. He wasn't a fan of confrontation. "You might have noticed that Sidney didn't find it very funny either."

"It's *Sidney*, now, is it?" Aiko had a distinctly irritable tone as she dropped to sit in the chair opposite his desk. "What the fuck, Weston? I thought you'd find it funny. Henry did."

"Well, it *wasn't*," Weston surprised himself by snapping. "Come on, you're not dumb. You know you can't throw friendly mocking at someone you're not friends with."

Aiko sneered. The expression didn't sit well on her face. "You think that was friendly? That was revenge for Moran."

"Revenge?" Weston sputtered. He'd stopped drawing altogether in favor of staring disbelievingly at Aiko. "What are you, thirteen years old? He was a drunk, Aiko. Everybody knew it; we just didn't act on it because nobody wants to fire someone in a small business like ours. Especially not someone with ties to Sanderson. Sidney was just doing his job."

Even as he said it, Weston felt surprise at his own words. It hadn't been that long since he'd been incredibly suspicious of Sidney too. The difference was, he'd actually made an effort to get to know the man.

"Doing his job by *firing* someone from theirs," Aiko replied.

"Doing the job that Sanderson hired him to." Weston shook his head. "He just made the suggestion. If you want to blame someone for booting Moran? Blame Sanderson. Or, hell, blame *Moran*, since he's the one who came into work hungover every day and barely got anything done."

Aiko still looked unhappy, but she didn't immediately shout back, which Weston took as a good sign. "It just sucks," she sighed then, her shoulders slumping. "We're like a little family here. I don't like losing anybody."

"Neither do I," Weston admitted. "But Sidney is passionate about his work. And I guess sometimes it can seem like he's a little harsh, but he has the best intentions in mind."

No, wait, that was Detective Saunders.

"I think," Weston amended.

"You sound like you're getting to know him pretty well." Aiko's eyes narrowed, her suspicion not entirely faded.

"Nah." Lying didn't come easy to Weston. "I mean, not really. I'm just good at people."

That made Aiko tip her head back and laugh. "Weston, you're *horrible* at people," she said. "I still remember at our last office Christmas party you tried to flirt by making animal noises."

"He was a zoologist," Weston defended himself. "He was interested!"

"He ran away. And he was dating Martha."

Weston gave a sigh of defeat. "Fine, I'm bad at people."

Aiko reached across the desk to give him a consoling pat on the hand. "You are," she agreed. "And maybe you're right about Moran. But I still don't trust the Leech. Ever since he walked through those doors, I've been triple-checking everything I do."

"Me too," Weston confessed. "But he seems like he wouldn't just randomly fire people who are actually good at their jobs."

"He'd better not. Otherwise the next mug will say a lot worse than 'I'm An Asshole'." Aiko frowned. "I wonder if they make worse messages than that on those mugs."

"What, like, 'I'm A Lamentably Detestable Imbecile Who Doesn't Know My Ass From My Elbow'?"

"I'm not sure that'd fit on the bottom of a mug."

"So just buy a regular mug and write it yourself," Weston suggested. "In very tiny handwriting. But only if Sidney deliberately destroys the company. Otherwise that insult's a bit too strong."

"Only you would think *that's* a strong insult," Aiko said with a roll of her eyes. "But fine. I'll reserve my opinion on the Leech, and I'll try to not hate him until he does something really bad."

"And could you maybe talk to Henry?" Weston hedged.

Aiko shook her head in disbelief. "Tell him yourself. I've actually got work to do. You know, unlike some people who just sit around doodling all day."

"I do not *doodle*," Weston protested. "Go away. You're destroying my Zen."

She laughed as she walked out the door, leaving Weston alone with his pile of paper, a cartoonish blue jay mascot staring back up at him.

Well, he'd cheered Sidney up and convinced Aiko to stop hating their productivity consultant. Weston felt as though he'd achieved a lot for the day.


WRITING continued not to go well after Weston got home.

He'd been sure, after his day, that he'd at least be able to write something. All that time with Sidney would surely poke the characters of Sentry and Saunders into life.

But there he was, slouched on his couch and staring blankly at the equally blank screen of his laptop.

"This is getting ridiculous," Weston muttered. "Just write something."

He decided Stephen and William, the overly dramatic romantic heroes, would make a return.

—◆——◆——◆——◆——◆——◆——◆——◆——◆——◆——◆——◆—

William collapsed against the plush couch. "*Le café, le lait, il est horrible*," he gushed happily. They had spent the day in the French countryside, surrounded by green hills and roaming sheep. It had been so romantic.

Stephen thoughtfully twiddled his moustache. *"La baguette avec fromage, la Tour Eiffel, la moustache."*

—•———•———•———•———•———•———•———•———•———•———•—

That might work better if Weston actually knew any French, instead of just listing French words he knew in place of dialogue.

He sighed, aggrieved, and deleted what he'd written.

He wasn't in the mood to write high fantasy *or* a detective story. The usual method was to try another genre, so Weston did. He grasped the first image that came to mind, and wrote:

—•———•———•———•———•———•———•———•———•———•———•—

Wirrex pointed his blaster at Captain Starson. "You shouldn't have come to this planet, Starson! Ipax-Four doesn't need your help!"

Starson held out a hand. "I only want to give aid. Come, my ship, Nova, is docked a short walk away from here. Don't you want to save your friends, Wirrex?"

Glancing nervously behind him, Wirrex eyed the blackness that was approaching. It was spreading over every plant and pebble like creeping death, coating everything in an oily blackness. In an hour, it would hit the city Xaridi, and it would evaporate everything it touched.

"What about everybody else? There are three hundred people here," Wirrex pleaded.

"I can only save a few," Starson said, his voice heavy with regret.

—•———•———•———•———•———•———•———•———•———•———•—

Weston stopped typing and tilted his head to the side as he reread what he'd just written.

It wasn't terrible. It wasn't *great*, either. He'd gotten far too into the stereotype of adding odd letters like X and Z to nearly every name to make them sound exotic and futuristic, but the idea wasn't bad in and of itself, even if the characters were stereotypical at best. Then again, it was only a small snippet.

"Huh," Weston said out loud. He couldn't quite get his head around the idea that he might have just written 124 words that weren't horrible, so he laboriously got himself upright, then headed toward the kitchen with the intention of making dinner.

Halfway through baking potatoes, he was still baffled at himself. Since he knew decent writing skills didn't just pop up out of nowhere, Weston assumed something must have happened to change how he wrote. There hadn't been the usual poking fun at the genre; he hadn't written the characters commenting on stereotypes.

Absently, Weston picked up his phone and sent a text to Henry: *Might have written something not complete drivel! Go me!*

Only after he sent it did he remember that he was supposed to be irritated at Henry for laughing at the mug gift, and Weston frowned down at his phone. If only there were some way to take back messages he'd sent. He wished he had Sidney's number—he would have sent that text to him instead.

Damn it. Sidney was supposed to be the productivity consultant and Henry the coworker-slash-friend. Weston didn't like it when things strayed out of their categories.

Determined to put that thought out of his mind, Weston ate dinner in front of his laptop. Though he didn't get any more writing done, he did order a few books. Perhaps some Asimov would inspire him into science fiction greatness.

# Chapter
## Eight

---•---•---•---•---•---•---•---•---•---•---•---

WIRREX'S hands shook as he gripped his blaster tighter, readjusting his hold to steady his aim. "Just leave," he barked. "Just turn around and leave."

The man had introduced himself as Captain Starson. He was wearing a Cardinal Prime regulation suit, the government uniform tight and sleek, black with silver lines running the length of his limbs. The helmet was melded to his head, flat in front of his face, leaving Wirrex staring at the beautiful vortex swirl of the glass. Unfortunately, it left him with no idea what Starson was thinking or feeling.

"You have two days before it reaches your city," Starson said bluntly. "I cannot take all of you; my ship's capacity is about fifty persons."

"We don't need your help, Cardinal Leech," Wirrex spat. "Go back to sucking the life out of other planets. This one's ours."

Starson sighed. Through the helmet, the sound was laced with static. "Then you will die upon it." He withdrew the hand he had held out. "You know where my ship is. I will stay planetside for two days." A green-and-gold spiral galaxy drifted over the glass, stars dotted white and yellow.

It was repulsive. A Cardinal Prime agent shouldn't wear something so beautiful.

Starson took his leave, walking back in the direction of his ship. Wirrex holstered his blaster, turned his back with only the slightest hesitation, then made for the city.

The city of Xaridi was old—*very* old. So old that none of the inhabitants knew where it had come from. It was clearly late thirty-third century in make, but by whom it had been built, none of them had been able to determine. Great metal pillars, rounded and rusted, reached into the dusky red sky, and for a moment, Wirrex could almost pretend that life was going on as usual. As he hit the city outskirts, he ducked a pair of laughing kids on a creaky old hoverboard. They blew past him fast enough to stir up the dust in the street.

At this time of day, in the middle of the afternoon, people were out and about in the central streets. The daily market was in full swing, the faded material of tent awnings rustling in the breeze. Men and women, young and old, displayed their wares, hoping to get even a few trades in return.

Wirrex ducked into a side street. At a faded old light sign bearing letters he did not know how to translate, he turned left and reached up the side of the building to grasp a metal rung. He climbed up the ladder and stood on the roof.

There, in the very distance, was blackness. A creeping, oily plague. It had taken the mountains. Soon it would hit the craggy plains, and from there, it would be two days until it reached Xaridi.

And yet the people of Xaridi still soldiered on, attempting to trade under the harsh beat of the midafternoon sun. Most of them clung stubbornly to the belief that the darkness would not hit them; it would stop before it took intelligent life, they argued.

Wirrex didn't agree.

He stepped closer to the edge of the roof, tugging his ragged shawl up to cover his nose and mouth as a dust cloud drifted past.

"Wirrex," a voice crackled in his ear. "You home yet?"

Reaching up to touch the slender piece of metal curled around his ear, Wirrex smiled. "Nearly, Halcor. I had a little run-in while I was gathering water. Everything okay?"

"Everything's fine. I—then—" The comm started crackling. "And—"

Wirrex shut it off with a sigh. Damn thing was always giving him trouble, and it wasn't exactly as though they had anybody to fix it, given that it was technology none of them were familiar with.

He climbed down to get back onto the street and walked past the vendors and the crowds. Some of the traders, the ones who offered the basics like food and blankets, traded the best. Others tried to make do with scavenged relics: weapons, comms, medical devices, and many other things that weren't identifiable. They didn't do too well.

Three hundred and twelve, their population was. They knew, through stories passed down, that a small group had settled on Ipax-Four six generations ago, though the knowledge of *why* had unfortunately been lost. Their records, as meager as they were, showed that the original settlers had come when Xaridi was already old and breaking, when the planet itself was hot, dusty, and barely livable.

Legend said Ipax-Four had once been a paradise. Unfortunately for the settlers, it had not been so when they'd arrived.

Wirrex pushed aside the cloth hanging that served as the door of his home—the actual door had long since broken off, and he had not been able to fix it. Halcor was seated on an old chair. "You look rattled," Halcor said. "Where were you?"

"There's a Cardinal Prime agent sitting outside the city."

"What?" Halcor yelped, jumping out of his seat. "What does he want?"

Wirrex just sighed. "I don't know. He said he could get some of us off the planet."

Halcor snorted. His hand, which had been drifting toward his gun, relaxed. "As if anybody would believe that," he grunted. "They're the ones who sent the plague in the first place."

"I should tell the elders," Wirrex supposed, heading toward the kitchen. His house was small, the metal walls interrupted by ribbed metal pipes climbing up the wall with what he assumed were numerals painted on them. The best he'd been able to determine was that this room was perhaps once part of a factory. It worked well enough as a shelter.

After finding two cups, Wirrex pushed aside a curtain on the window to bring more light in. "They'll want to know, won't they?"

"I doubt they'll believe you," Halcor muttered, sitting back down. Dark-haired and tall, he dwarfed the chair as he idly scratched at a neatly trimmed beard. "They think it'll stop. I bet they think Cardinal Prime *hasn't* done this to other planets before too."

"Have they?" Wirrex questioned, taking a pinch of herbs from a jar and sprinkling it into the mugs. "We don't exactly have off-world communication."

"What, are you on Prime's side now?" Halcor glared at him.

"No, of course not." Wirrex laughed quietly as he filled a pot with water. "I'm just reminding you that although we think the plague won't stop until it's killed us all, we have as much proof as the elders do for their opinion. We've never seen this before."

Halcor sagged back into his seat, digging into his pocket to find his clock. "Well, you need to tell *someone* about the Cardinal Leech that apparently wants to help us."

"I just told you." Wirrex did his very best to look innocent.

"Doesn't count." Halcor gave him a withering glare.

"I know." Wirrex ducked his head to focus on the herb tea he was making. "I must tell the elders. Even if they don't believe me, they will recognize the importance of a choice for the people here." Even if it was only fifty of them allowed.

"Good." Halcor stood, pocketing his clock. "And now that I've made sure you're back safely, I need to go back to the mines."

Wirrex frowned, disappointed. "But I just made you herb tea!"

"So keep it cold and I'll come around tonight for it." Halcor grinned.

Wirrex sighed at him. "It's not as good cold. But all right. You'd better show up. You know how the elders get on our case if we waste water."

Halcor tipped his hat at Wirrex. "Message received."

He left with a rustle of the cloth at the doorway, a thump as he tread on the slightly loose stair, and Wirrex was alone again, left to stare out the window at the approaching sickness.

FOUR hours later, just as the sun was beginning to touch the horizon, Wirrex banged at the door of Starson's ship. From the sleek and shiny paneling of it, it was clearly a new make, the date of construction carved in small letters under the name. *Nova*. Wirrex had never particularly been interested in ships, but he could admit that this was a beautiful one, even if it was government property.

"Starson!" he yelled. "I need to talk to you!"

He stepped backward in a hurry as the door made a hissing sound, descending to lie flat on the ground in a small ramp. Starson was there, suit still on.

"Have you decided to come with me?" the man said, his voice suffering only the slightest of crackling through the helmet.

"I need you to tell me if the darkness will kill everyone," Wirrex said. "Some of the elders believe it won't. They think it will stop before it reaches the city. But you said it will take it over. I need the truth."

Starson didn't say anything for a long time. That slowly twisting galaxy of glass was impossible to read, and Wirrex wondered if it meant anything—if the drifting appearance of a yellow planet in the corner reflected what Starson thought or if it was just random. "Come with me," Starson finally said, taking a few steps back to let Wirrex walk inside the ship.

It was as beautiful inside as it was outside—gleaming white metal in smooth curves. They walked in silence until they reached the cockpit, where Starson's gloved hands moved over a screen and brought up a picture of Ipax-Four.

"This is where the Life is now," he said.

"The what?"

Starson tilted his head. "The Life. That is its name. Do you know what it does?"

Wirrex had to shake his head. "We saw that it killed whatever it touched."

"It does." A cluster of bright stars drifted over the helmet. Perhaps that was a smile? "It obliterates everything. And when everything is dead, then new life can begin again, once Cardinal Prime sows the seeds."

"But there's *already* life here!" Wirrex protested.

"Cardinal Prime is aware. But you are unregistered, and that is a crime punishable by death." Starson's shoulders slumped slightly. "I... find myself in the unusual position of not agreeing with what I have been ordered to do."

He moved his hand, showing the picture of Ipax-Four. Around half of it was the darkness—the Life—and when Starson tapped the screen, the black continued moving. "This is what the Life will do."

Wirrex watched as it slowly stole over the planet, covering the city inch by inch, dissolving it to the ground.

Then, as the black receded, green began to grow in its place. "Legend says that this planet used to be a paradise," Wirrex said lowly. "Are they trying to remake it?"

"Yes." Starson swiped over the screen, and the picture vanished. "But I do not think I can stand idly by while more than three hundred people get...."

"Get what?" Wirrex couldn't help but ask. "What happens when the Life touches a living thing? We only saw the desert *duna* die from a great distance."

"It is not a nice death." Starson sounded as though he was grimacing. "The Life touches them, and their cells simply... lose cohesion. It returns nutrients to the earth."

Wirrex had to turn aside as he swallowed down the sour taste at the back of his throat. If he could hear the disgust in Starson's voice, it must be strong. It must be a terrible thing to witness.

"I don't know if I can trust you," he said frankly. "How am I to know that you won't rescue us only to shuttle us right to some central planet jail?"

Starson made a sound that might have been a dry laugh. "Do you recognize my insignia?"

Wirrex glanced back at him, at the badge he was pointing to on his chest. It was a circle with a hexagon shape inside, a neatly printed cluster of five planets in a semicircle. "No," he admitted. "I don't."

"I'm part of the Isolated Lifeforms Protection division. It's my job to ensure that small colonies prosper." Starson shook his head. "*Registered* small colonies. I've spent most of my life helping people exactly like yours. Now my superiors want me to monitor the terraforming of a planet and expect me to sit idly by while people die. I can't do that."

Wirrex stared silently out the front window of the ship. Though he didn't know much about Cardinal Prime, he knew they didn't take too kindly to their own agents disobeying direct orders. Yet here Starson was, offering to take as many people as he could off-planet to save them.

"What will happen to you if you do this?" he asked.

There was a smile in Starson's voice. "Do not worry about that. Worry instead about your people. You said there were elders?"

"Yes, and I should inform them." Wirrex restrained the urge to fidget with the console in front of him. "They will know what to do. You should come with me so that they don't think I'm making things up."

"Of course." Starson tilted his head in agreement. "Lead the way."

The walk back to the city was dry, dusty, and hot, and they climbed over stretches of craggy rock to get there. Starson seemed to study some in particular, staring at them as long as he could, but he made no mention as to why he was doing it. Wirrex just supposed the man might be interested in rocks; who knew?

There were fewer people on the streets now, only a few still around to stare curiously at Starson as he and Wirrex walked toward the center of the city. Some were not so curious, their expressions suspicious, hateful.

The elders resided in the grandest building of Xaridi, the Dome. The Dome was used as their greenhouse, the only environment in which they could grow vegetation for consumption, as few but the hardiest plants survived out in the rocky deserts. It was a long-standing tradition that the elders resided with the heart of the city. Some joked that the heart was where the food was, but it was life that they surrounded themselves with, life in a harsh, arid land.

The elders sat at a large semicircle table, clearly expecting them. Some said that the eldest, both ancient and wise, had vision beyond that of the common person. Judge, they called her.

"Take off your mask, law man," Judge said as they approached the table.

"I suspect you can already see through it, elder," Starson replied. "But I will remove it."

With two gloved hands, he reached up and clasped either side of the helmet. With a snap and a hiss, it released the lock to the suit. The swirl of galaxies on glass faded to dull black as Starson lifted the helmet free.

Wirrex knew it was impolite to stare, but he could not help it. Starson was more handsome than he expected.

"You bring us news of the plague." Judge leaned forward, her necklaces shifting against each other. "Tell us."

"It is going to claim your city." The other elders murmured amongst themselves at Starson's words. "Wirrex tells me that you do not believe it will, but I have seen this before. Cardinal Prime wants to restore Ipax-Four to its original fertility, and they care not for the unregistered persons already inhabiting it."

Another elder, Aili, scowled. "And what has Cardinal Prime sent you to do? Watch us die?"

"That was their intention." Starson looked grave, his dark eyes downcast. "But I cannot do that. My job is to protect small colonies, not watch them be massacred." He squared his shoulders, standing tall. "I have a ship, elders. I can offer fifty people an escape off this planet."

"Only fifty?" Another elder gasped. "But what of the rest of us?"

"That is all I can offer." Starson seemed unhappier about this than even the elders did.

Aili slammed a fist on the table. "We are not saving only *some* of us," she growled. "You must talk to your superiors. You *must* make them spare us."

"I have tried." Starson shook his head slowly. "They refused. I contacted other agents in my division, but they will not help. You have my deepest apologies."

"But we are a community of many more than a mere *fifty* people," Aili argued.

"I am sorry, elder." Starson's frown was small but deeply apologetic. "If I was being absolutely safe, I would recommend forty. It is a fifteen-day trip from here to the nearest planet. Fifty people is pushing it."

"If fifty is all you can offer, then that is what we will take," Judge said evenly.

Aili raised her voice in protest, as did another elder. Two others started arguing with her, seemingly forgetting Starson and Wirrex's presence.

In the chaos at the table, Wirrex studied Starson once more. He looked to be from a border planet, with his olive skin and black hair, high cheekbones giving him a sharp face. A hint of stubble shadowed his jaw, and the creases at the corner of his eyes made him appear tired. It was nice to see his face instead of the glass of the helmet.

"Do you think they will agree?" Starson's murmured words brought Wirrex out of his thoughts.

"I don't know," Wirrex said honestly. "I really don't know."

Hours later, the elders had reached a decision.

Starson and Wirrex had gone to sit at the edge of the room to watch the elders debate. They had talked lowly between themselves, and Starson had shared stories of his home planet—Wirrex had come to very much like that gleam of fondness in Starson's eyes, the smile that curled at his lips when he thought of home. In return, Wirrex had done the same, telling Starson all about life on Ipax-Four—how he'd grown up with his mother; about Halcor, his best friend; about his job gathering water and finding springs.

Wirrex was smiling at Starson when the elders fell silent, and he turned to look at them. Judge's hands lay clasped on the table, and beside them was a list.

"Fifty of us will go," Judge said. "This list was made in haste, for we have little time, but we made it to the best of our judgment."

It hadn't even occurred to Wirrex that he might *not* be one of the fifty who flew safely away with Starson. As he looked, he saw that the list did not bear his name.

Cold dread formed in the pit of his stomach. He was doomed to die here, to be overtaken by the darkness and die a terrible death. He could not argue with the elders' decision.

"We have chosen the strongest, the most skilled, and most fertile of us." Judge was still talking. "Those who will have the best chance of rebuilding our community elsewhere."

Wirrex felt numb. He looked at the list again. It did not bear Judge's name either.

"But, elder, why are *you* not on the list?" he managed, his voice faint. "I see all four elders, but not you."

"I am old." Judge smiled gently. "And my time has passed. I would not take up a spot on that ship when a younger, more able person can go."

Wirrex felt tears sting the back of his eyes, and he clenched his jaw, determined to get rid of them. "I will inform those on the list of what they have to do," he decided.

Wirrex walked out, unwilling to let any of them see his face. When he reached the entrance of the building, he nearly collapsed, his legs going weak underneath him. Two days. Two more days was all he had left to live. Many of the people of Xaridi had suspected they did not have long before the darkness consumed them all, but there had been hope. Hope that Cardinal Prime would see the error of its ways and stop their plague before it hit, or take them off the planet. The latter would only need one of their bigger ships.

But here they were. Fifty people to be saved. Two hundred sixty-two people would die.

He heard steps coming up behind him. "Were you not on the list?" There was concern in Starson's voice.

Slowly, Wirrex shook his head. "No. My name was not there."

Starson looked pained. "I wish that was not so," he said, grief lining his words. "I wish I had the clearance to bring a bigger ship."

"You are already doing an amazing thing," Wirrex told him. "You will be saving fifty of us. And I do not know what punishment will be given to you for disobeying direct orders, but I know that you are a good man for doing this."

He reached out to touch Starson's arm, trying to reassure him. Starson's expression softened at the contact. "It is not enough," Starson repeated quietly.

Wirrex attempted a smile for him. "It has to be."

THE next day shepherded in a dull morning and a dusty afternoon full of telling some that they would live, and some that they would die. Wirrex hated the job, but as he felt as though it was his responsibility, he didn't pass it off on to someone else.

Starson stayed with him the whole time, helmet in place. Some residents of Xaridi screamed at him, blaming him. Some wept. Some hit him, and Starson bore it all in steely silence.

When night came, Wirrex wound up at the *Nova*. The cargo bay was in the back of the ship, which was where Wirrex and Starson were currently seated. The large access ramp stretched before them, open to the night air as they sat on the floor, two mugs of herb tea placed in front of them.

Wirrex wasn't sure he'd managed to comprehend what was happening. He kept thinking about it, of course. As he'd stopped by his home, he'd thought about how he'd spent so long fixing it up and making it livable, only to soon have it destroyed. He'd laughed helplessly at his stack of tea, painstakingly gathered so that he would not run out for months; he never would have thought he needn't have spent the time. But despite those thoughts, despite those realizations, he didn't think he'd completely grasped the concept that he would die the next day.

Halcor was not on the list either. In an unforgivable display of weakness, Wirrex had not been able to tell him of his fate. He and

Starson had lingered in front of Halcor's door, though they'd never made it inside.

"The night sky here is beautiful," Starson murmured. "It's a much clearer view than what I get at home."

"There is only the one major city," Wirrex replied, smiling faintly. "Unlike the central planets. I hear they are just one big city."

Starson, without his helmet now, laughed. "That may be a slight exaggeration."

Wrapping both hands around his mug to ward off the chill, Wirrex admitted, "I'd hoped to visit one of them one day. We don't know much about the outside galaxy here, because we don't have the technology to travel. But I'd hoped…."

"Stow away on the ship," Starson said suddenly. "I'll hide you, if need be."

Wirrex felt hope bloom and die in his chest in a matter of seconds. "I can't," he said softly. "You said it yourself. The ship only holds fifty."

"*Nova*'s capacity will only host fifty at a risky stretch," Starson said, staring intently at Wirrex. "I've calculated for air and food supplies. We will need to eat lighter and make sure we do not do anything strenuous. Fifty-one… if I burn a bit more fuel than I normally dare, then we could make it."

"But you could take another in my place. Someone more capable, someone more useful to a rebuilding society."

All day, they had bolstered each other's spirits by telling silly childhood stories. Wirrex had told Starson of growing up on the planet, of exploring the rusted old wreck of the edge of the city, the way his mother had constantly despaired for his safety.

He'd told Starson that he admired him for standing there while those who would die raged at him. Though it was an impossible situation, Starson had recognized that they needed a target, someone to blame, even though he was sacrificing something himself too. Starson had smiled and told Wirrex he had been born in a small colony much like Ipax-Four. Helping them was his passion.

"I don't want to take anybody else," Starson said lowly.

Wirrex turned his head. They were so close. If Wirrex moved an inch to the left, Starson's shoulder would be pressed against his. Despite the cold night air, he was sure he could feel heat crackling between them.

Falling in love with someone of the same gender was generally not encouraged on Ipax-Four, not when their numbers were so low. But Wirrex had never looked at a woman the same way he looked at men. He knew he had no hope of ever falling for a member of the opposite gender.

And here was this man, this brave, courageous man… and Wirrex was falling for him.

Just the thought of it made heat rise to his cheeks. He was by no means a virgin; it was more the ridiculousness of it all. A man he'd only known for a day and a half? He should not be experiencing this kind of emotion for him. He was probably going to *die*. Feelings were futile.

But Starson was offering him a place on the ship.

"Are you sure that I won't endanger the rescue mission?" Wirrex asked, tentatively hopeful.

"I will see to it that everybody gets safely onto another planet," Starson promised. "All fifty-one of you."

Wirrex didn't know who moved first, him or Starson, but they were kissing then, a clash of lips that was nearly bruising. He was so grateful that it felt as though he was kissing Starson with all of that emotion bursting within him, and for the first few long moments, it was bliss.

Until he drew back, embarrassed. "I'm sorry," he managed. "That was rude of me."

Starson's eyes were darker than usual. "Not at all," he said huskily and drew Wirrex into another kiss. This one was gentler, more explorative, and the chill of the night ceased to matter as they pressed close. Wirrex moved his hand to Starson's shoulder, tugging him nearer, and as he shifted his legs, he knocked over one of the mugs of herb tea with a splash. He attempted to ignore it, but he could feel Starson grinning against his lips.

"Clumsy." Starson said warmly, bringing his hand up to cup Wirrex's jaw. "Say you'll come with me."

"I'll come with you," Wirrex replied. "But I have no way to repay you for saving my life."

"You don't need to." Starson's fingers smoothed through the hair at Wirrex's nape. "Of course you don't need to." He paused then and smirked. "But if you *want* to, I'll take your thanks in the form of more kisses."

Wirrex laughed, feeling lighter than he had in days. "I'll see to it that your kindness is repaid in full, then," he murmured, and their lips met again.

THE next day was not nearly so nice. From the moment the sun rose, Starson projected that they had eight hours until the Life started destroying Xaridi.

The people knew they were doomed now. Some accepted it, but others did not.

And Wirrex had to tell his best friend he had not made it onto the list.

Halcor's home was a little larger than his own, set on the second floor of a tall spire. Those who worked dangerous jobs, the elders said, deserved good houses. It was made of metal, like most dwellings in the city—and since Halcor labored in the mines, it was roomier than most homes, and structurally more sound.

When Wirrex stepped through the door, he saw Halcor sitting at the lone table, a stone carving clutched between his hands. "I noticed that you didn't get around to telling me anything yesterday," Halcor said, his voice faint.

"I know." Wirrex grit his teeth. "I'm... I'm so sorry, Halcor. I didn't know what to say."

Halcor had been his friend through thick and thin. When both of their fathers had died in the mines, they'd had each other. For a long time, Wirrex had wished he could love Halcor. Sadly, Halcor was straight, though he was yet unwed. Wirrex owed his friend a lot.

Now he had to leave him to die.

"And you?" Halcor raised damp eyes to Wirrex, a morbid hope in them. "Are you going to be here too, to make my death a little less lonely?"

Wirrex swallowed around a lump in his throat. Starson was standing just outside, away from Halcor's view. Walking closer to Halcor so that he could sit opposite him, Wirrex reached out to fold his hands over his friend's. "I wasn't on the list," he confessed. "But Starson, he... he offered me a place."

"Then take me too." Halcor's eyes had a wild, desperate look in them. "Wirrex, please, you have to convince him to take me too. I don't want to die."

Starson stepped just inside the door. "Even one more will make a difference," he said lowly, apologetic. "I cannot take you too."

"Why *not*?" Halcor cried. "One more surely would not matter that much."

"I'm pushing it with offering to take fifty, Halcor." Starson spoke gently, but his words were firm. "Do you know how much air the average person breathes in a day? My ship has only a limited capacity—305,000 cubic feet of air. Over the fifteen-day trip, fifty plus myself will breathe 296,000 cubic feet. Adding one more passenger makes it dangerous. Adding *two* more...." Starson took a deep breath, shaking his head. "That would put us over capacity. We wouldn't make it, even with every precaution taken. Two more, and we damn everybody on the ship."

"Halcor can take my place," Wirrex offered, stumbling over his words in his haste to say them. He couldn't bear the look of upset on his best friend's face. "He can go instead of me."

Halcor stood and paced a short distance away from them. He went to stare out the window to watch the community pack their belongings. "Wirrex," he started.

"I'm not really that useful anyway, right?" Wirrex tried to sound upbeat, forcing a smile. "If we only get fifty-one people to rebuild our entire culture, then one of them should be you."

He saw Halcor pass a hand over his face, then rub at his forehead. The tense line of his shoulders spoke far more than words ever could. "No," Halcor said finally. "You should go."

"No," Wirrex protested. "We'll both stay, then. I'm not leaving you to die alone, Halcor."

"And either way, you're damning yourself to die." Halcor turned to face them again, his expression grave. "I'm not okay with that."

"But—"

"Why me?" Halcor gave Wirrex a faint, hopeless smile. "Why not Blazit from down the road? Why not Eltor, the man who fixes my cooker?"

Wirrex had no good answer. He wanted to say, *Because you're my friend*, but even before he said it, he knew it wasn't a good reason. Blazit had friends and family too, as did Eltor. As did everybody who would die.

"Either one of you lives," Starson broke in gently, "or two of you die, Wirrex."

"And Starson asked *you*." Halcor still sounded unhappy. "I don't want to die, but I'm not going to ask you to die, either, and I'm not going to force my way on and damn us all. So go with him, Wirrex."

"Damn it," Wirrex whispered. He felt so guilty for being relieved that he still had a chance to live. He was no more important than the ones who had not been chosen, but at the same time, his life was worth every bit as much as everybody else's.

Starson put a hand on Wirrex's shoulder. "Time is running short," he said lowly.

"I don't know what to say," Wirrex admitted to Halcor. He wanted to insist Halcor be the one to go, but it looked like Halcor had made up his mind.

Halcor smiled that hopeless smile again. "How about you say you'll erect a massive memorial for me on whatever planet you get to?"

Despite the guilt and the pain, Wirrex laughed. "I promise. I'll even write a praising poem." He reached out and clasped Halcor's forearms. "I won't forget you."

As he hugged Halcor in farewell, Wirrex did his best to remain calm. His friend didn't need him collapsing in hysterics. His last sight of Halcor was the man's tenuous smile as Wirrex and Starson walked out.

Starson guided Wirrex through throngs of panicked people in the street. Until Wirrex stumbled, his foot catching on a stray piece of debris, and Wirrex sank to the ground on his knees, trying to stop the tears from trickling down his cheeks.

Starson immediately knelt with him, grabbing him in an embrace. "I'm sorry," he said. "I'm sorry I can't take him with us. I'm so sorry."

"He's my best friend," Wirrex gasped, his breath hitching. His face pressed painfully against Starson's shoulder. "And I have to leave him to die. I can't do this."

"You can," Starson said gently. He hooked two fingers underneath Wirrex's chin and tilted his face up to look up at him. Around them, people flowed in a nervous rhythm, some gathering their belongings, most wandering aimlessly. "It will be hard. It will be the hardest thing you've ever done. But you will be alive."

"I feel so selfish," Wirrex muttered, swiping his sleeve across his eyes. "Is it selfish of me? To feel happy that I will live?"

Starson brushed a thumb over Wirrex's cheek. His smile was sad. "No. It's just instinct."

Wirrex was reluctant to break their embrace, even if they were kneeling on dusty ground in the middle of the street. Looking up into Starson's eyes, he felt as though everything would be okay in the end, though it would take a long time to get there. Their society would be able to rebuild.

"Thank you," Wirrex whispered. "I don't know why you offered to take me. But thank you."

"Is it really not that obvious?" Amidst the mess of people, Starson leaned down to kiss Wirrex's forehead. There was a confused glint in his eye, but he looked fond. "I've never fallen for someone quite so fast. But then you aimed a blaster at my head, and I saw your strength. Your passion when you thought you were defending your people."

Wirrex stood with Starson's help. He laughed shakily. "I threatened you with a weapon and you liked me on sight? I think that makes you a masochist."

"Perhaps." Starson's smile was fond, a little sly. "Now, are you ready to pack your belongings?"

Wirrex couldn't look back at Halcor's dwelling as they left. His eyes were still burning with every step farther away from his best friend. But Starson was going to save him. He was going to *live*. And he couldn't be more grateful.

WITH fifty-two people onboard, the *Nova* lifted smoothly into the sky. Only fifty-two people of Xaridi, with as many belongings as they could pack. The four remaining elders made sure to bring items of importance: history books, seeds from the Dome, art works that had long been admired, crafts and weavings. Anything of their own that they could fit into the ship, anything unique to their society.

The relics of the city, the strange machinery their people had not made, were largely left behind.

Those were the things Wirrex could not help but think about as the ship rumbled underneath his feet, as he watched the city appear to grow smaller. The people there before them, the puzzles they had never been able to figure out—he was sad most of them would be wiped out. For all he knew, that city was the only thing left standing of those who had lived there before.

He didn't want them to be forgotten. Wirrex had taken his earpiece and a few sketches of the city he'd made years ago. He hoped that he would one day be able to find somebody who knew who had once populated Ipax-Four.

Starson's steps were quiet behind him. The man came to a stop beside Wirrex, who noticed the ship was motionless in the air, the engines purring as it hovered.

"I didn't want anybody to have to watch this," Starson said. His helmet was off, his features creased in sympathy. "But the elders requested it."

They stood to watch as the black Life crept ever closer to the city. Once at its borders, it seemed to pick up speed, as if sensing there was something to be eradicated. Wirrex closed his eyes briefly, thankful that they were a little too high up to see people. He knew some would be running, attempting to escape it. Halcor was probably still in his house.

Like a wave, the Life swept over Xaridi. Numb with horror, Wirrex watched as the towers seemed to melt, buckling at the bottom and falling into the plague, steel swirling gray over the black before vanishing entirely.

Starson had been right. Things didn't die in the Life. They simply lost cohesion.

Wirrex was only dimly aware of the tears on his cheeks. Starson's arm rested over his shoulders, and together they watched Xaridi succumb to blackness. The weeping of the other fifty people was audible from the deck below.

"Where will you take us?" he managed to ask.

"I will leave the decision up to your elders, but I thought my home planet might be a good fit," Starson replied lowly, pulling Wirrex closer against his side. "It's beautiful; I think you'll like it there."

Wirrex smiled through his tears, turning to look at Starson. "Will you be there?" He knew Cardinal Prime did not take lightly to its agents disobeying orders, but in Starson's case, he had just rescued as many people as he could. Despite their unregistered status, Wirrex was sure that Starson would remain free.

"I aim to be." Starson pressed a kiss to his forehead. "And if they want to lock me up for saving lives, I suppose I shall simply have to be on the run."

"You'd do that for us?"

"Yes." Starson drew back to look at Wirrex, solemn. "I would do it for *you*."

--+----+----+----+----+----+----+----+----+----+--

# Chapter Nine

THE phone was ringing.

Struggling out from under his messy pile of sheets, Weston picked it up. "Hello?" he grunted into it.

"Weston!" Sidney said cheerfully from the other end of the line. "I'm sorry, I know it's early."

"Huh?" Weston stared blankly at the ceiling.

Sidney laughed. "Are you not a morning person?"

"Ugh," Weston replied. "Sidney?"

He blinked at the ceiling. Once. Twice. And then remembered his dream.

Oh, Christ. Another Sidney clone, except that one had been called Starson and….

He'd had a sex dream about Sidney. Okay, not a sex dream. And not really Sidney. But a kissing dream about a guy who looked exactly like Sidney and had some of his qualities.

"You saved me," he said groggily.

"Pardon?" Sidney sounded bemused.

Weston had enough brainpower to hold his tongue. "Never mind. Why are you calling at… I don't even know what time it is."

"Oh, I, er." Sidney's words sounded hesitant. "I don't know. I just wanted to see how you were."

"At the asscrack of dawn? You'll see me in two hours."

"Yes. I suppose I will."

Weston gave a groan as his eyes fell shut again. "Going back to sleep now," he mumbled. "Bye."

He heard the call click off, and let himself slowly drift back to sleep with an absent smile on his face.

An hour later, his alarm jolted him awake—but instead of the usual irritation Weston found himself with upon waking, he was still smiling. He remembered, after a few hazy moments, that Sidney had called him for no reason at all.

That struck him as kind of sweet, even though it had been ridiculously early, and Weston did not use the word *sweet* lightly.

The smile remained even as he hauled himself out of bed to start getting ready for work. Weston was not used to looking in the mirror and seeing himself look *happy* in the mornings—that was definitely an unusual sight.

As he worked on his breakfast, he idly typed notes from his dream, but he found he couldn't focus. All Weston could think about was the swirl of galaxies on glass—and that kiss.

God, that kiss.

Even just the memory of that moment in the dream made him smile. Sure, the romance in the dream had been a bit stereotypical—Weston wasn't a fan of characters falling in love at first sight; it seemed so unrealistic—but it had felt so real. Wirrex's love for Starson... he'd *felt* it, and he carried the memory of the feeling even now as he was glancing over the morning headlines.

But Starson was Sidney. Sentry, Saunders—they'd been Sidney too. Not completely the same, but they'd held aspects of the man. His appearance, his dry sense of humor, the little smile that tugged at his lips.

And now, as Weston thought about seeing Sidney at the office, that dreamed emotion made a reappearance.

"Shit," Weston said out loud, staring at his notes. "*Shit.*"

HE COULDN'T look Sidney in the eye at the office.

Sentry, Saunders, Starson. He'd loved them, in those dreams. No, that wasn't right. WingBlade, Wickham, and Wirrex had loved those men, not Weston. But they *were* Weston, and the other characters were Sidney.

His head was starting to hurt.

Determined to think about something else, Weston put his head down to work. His fixed tablet had been delivered, and that provided a good distraction as he got used to it again, relearning how the stylus moved over the smooth surface. He was so focused on it that he missed his morning coffee run, only to have Aiko deliver it with a bemused look on her face and an expectation of a tip.

Sidney walked past the glass wall of his office once, clearly busy. But when Weston was carefully putting the detail in the blue jay costume, Sidney knocked.

"Gah!" Weston's stylus made a huge arc across the screen.

"Sorry!" Sidney said, looking startled himself. "Sorry, I didn't mean to scare you."

"No, it's, uh, it's fine." Weston erased the line, exhaling slowly. "My fault, I was deep in art mode." He glanced up at Sidney's shoulder. "What can I do for you?"

There was a smile in Sidney's reply. "I know how terrible the coffee is here, so I brought you some from down the road." He set a paper coffee cup on Weston's desk.

Sidney was so thoughtful. Just like Saunders had been.

"Thanks," Weston mumbled.

"Are you okay?" Sidney sounded concerned. Weston couldn't see it in his expression, because he was very determinedly not looking at it. "I didn't wake you up too early with my phone call, did I?"

"No, no, I went right back to sleep." Weston took the lid off the cup and blew onto the steaming coffee. "It's okay. But seriously, that was *early*. Why were you even up that early?"

"Well, I can't come in an hour *late* after my morning workout," Sidney said dryly. "So I have to get up early for it."

"You work out?" Of course Sidney did. Weston bet he looked just as good as Sentry had. Sentry had worn very few clothes and had had the sort of body that would make ancient Greek sculptors weep for joy. "That sounds... exhausting."

He heard Sidney laugh. "Not a fan?"

"God, no." Weston shuddered. "The only exercise I get is walking on my lunch break."

Sidney settled into the chair across the desk, and Weston's eyes met his. He liked Sidney's eyes; they were dark in this light, as intelligent as Starson's had been.

"So, what did you mean this morning?" Sidney asked, curious. "You said I saved you?"

Weston wasn't a man overly given to blushing, but he came very close right then. "I was dreaming," he apologized.

"About what?"

"Uh, nothing really." Weston rubbed the back of his neck, embarrassed. "I don't really remember. Maybe you pulled me out of a fire?"

Sidney's expression tightened instead of the smile Weston was expecting. "Actually, about that, there was something I wanted to tell you."

Weston raised his eyebrows. "Was that why you called this morning?"

"Oh, no." Sidney ducked his head. "That was unrelated. I just felt the urge to call you."

The grin Weston hadn't been able to stop all morning came back in force. "No complaints from me."

Sidney looked pleased. "Really? I was sure I was being obnoxious."

"Hell no. It was nice."

Sentry. Saunders. Starson. That warmth in the pit of his stomach. Weston had been on the verge of starting to like Sidney before that latest dream; he'd started noticing how handsome the man was, how kind and strong. But now those feelings had bloomed into something so much stronger.

"In any case, I was talking to Sanderson this morning as I arrived." Sidney's words were hesitant. "He told me to run all of your work reports. He wants to massively cut down on employees."

"What?" Weston felt all of that warmth drain out of him, replaced with a cold numbness tainted with nervousness. "But there's only twenty-three of us. We barely have multiple divisions; I think there's about four. How many jobs is he going to cut?"

"I don't know," Sidney said apologetically. "I don't think I should even be telling you this, but I had to."

"Fuck," Weston whispered. "I can't believe he'd do that. He hasn't fired anybody in about five years." Except for Moran. From what Sidney said, that was clearly only the start of it. But Sanderson had always preached the values of small business, of keeping loyal employees and rewarding them for their hard work. He'd always been a vocal big corporation hater, disliking the way they offshored jobs and cut people out just to make a fraction more profit.

A week ago he would have blamed Sidney for this. But Sidney was just the man Sanderson had hired to get a second opinion.

"I hate being a part of this," Sidney admitted heavily. "Please believe me when I tell you that."

"I do." Weston reached over without thinking about it and put his hand on the arm Sidney had laid on the desk. "I know." He felt Sidney jerk a little in surprise, but he didn't withdraw his arm.

"Helping small businesses was the reason I became a productivity consultant." Sidney sighed, though there was a little smile in the corner of his eyes as he looked at Weston's hand. It soon vanished when he continued speaking. "Not tearing them apart."

"Is there anything you can do?" Weston asked. "You could save us, Sidney."

He'd saved Weston from the darkness, after all. The Life. The oily black plague that—

No, that had been Starson. Damn it, Weston needed to stop getting confused. Maybe he also needed to stop eating cheese before he slept—didn't some people say that doing that gave people vivid dreams? But that utter faith in Sidney remained. He was sure Sidney could save them. He was charismatic and brave and resourceful like that.

"There you go, talking about saving again," Sidney said ruefully. "I'm not sure how much I can do, Weston. But I can try."

"I know you can do it." Weston squeezed Sidney's arm. He then realized he was still touching Sidney and removed his hand with a nervous smile. "Sorry. I didn't mean to get all up in your personal space."

"It's quite okay." Sidney looked a little nervous himself. "In fact, I wanted to ask you something."

Weston couldn't help a laugh. "You have a lot on your agenda today."

"Apparently." Sidney returned his smile. "I wanted to ask if you'd have drinks with me. Tonight."

Weston nearly agreed automatically. His first instinct was that it was some kind of business meeting with drinks, and of course he'd have business drinks. But he was evidently a little slow that morning, because it took a few seconds for the puzzle pieces to connect. The phone call, the coffee, Sidney telling him the boss's plans when he probably shouldn't, the nervous little look Sidney was wearing now.

Sidney had just asked him out on a date.

Or, maybe not a *date* date. But it was definitely non-business related. Maybe like a predate, the sort of meeting you had with someone when you wanted to determine if you wanted to date them.

Weston should probably stop mentally freaking out.

"Fuck yes," he blurted. "I mean. Yes, I'd like to."

"Fuck yes worked just fine." Sidney smiled hopefully.

"I mean, this is a date, right?" Weston felt the need to clarify. "Otherwise it'd be really awkward if you were just proposing friendly drinks and I was thinking it was a date."

Sidney raised an eyebrow, bemused. "It is a date, yes."

"Then I'll say it again: fuck yes." Weston beamed. "When and where?"

His heart was doing that nervous, fluttery thing inside his chest, and Weston had to remind himself that flailing—no, *expansive gesturing*—wasn't an option. His last partner had broken up with him because of all the nervous expansive gesturing and hysteria, so he'd said, and Weston was going to do a lot better this time.

"How about that bar on the corner of North Street, at eight?" Sidney looked a little nervous too, which made Weston feel better.

"Perfect." Oh God, he'd have to dress himself. Weston had never been very good at dressing himself. Maybe he could call Henry or Judy? No, they'd just laugh at him. Aiko, then? No, he was still kind of pissed off at Aiko. And maybe a little at Henry too, considering he'd advocated the terrible gift idea. Weston officially had nobody to give him advice. "Fair warning, I may look terrible."

"You never look terrible." Sidney smiled, standing from the chair. "I'll see you at eight?"

"It's a date." Weston mentally congratulated himself for both the rhyme and the tying in of stereotypical sayings that actually applied right then. Maybe he could use that in his writing somewhere.

HE WOUND up calling Henry.

"I'm still a little pissed at you for the stupid mug prank, but I need your help," Weston said into the phone. After getting home from work, he'd promptly thrown the entirety of his wardrobe's contents on his bed and had spent half an hour despondently staring.

"What a nice way to say hello," Henry said dryly. He didn't sound too happy either.

Weston wasn't used to fighting with Henry. It made him upset, and he hated feeling upset. It also made him feel a little guilty, as though it was his fault—he knew it wasn't, but the feeling remained nonetheless.

But Henry's voice made him remember Halcor in his dream, the way he'd collapsed, sobbing messily, when he'd found out he was going to die alone.

That guilt in Weston's stomach gave a sharp clench.

"Sorry," Weston mumbled. "I'm not *really* mad."

"Weston, I love you and all, but we're so not having this conversation over a phone." Henry's voice had the distinct sound of an eye roll to it. "Or at all, actually. You might be all emotions and hugs, but I solve conflicts with beer and meat."

"And hopefully fire applied to the latter," Weston said. "So can you come over?"

"This isn't a booty call, is it?" Henry sounded suspicious. "I still remember your weird fantasy dream with HardDick or whatever it was."

"Hard*Iron*, Henry." Weston gave a long-suffering sigh. "And you were my dwarf companion."

Henry gave a groan. "Okay, just stop. I'm coming over. Christ, just don't talk about 'companions' or hard anything anymore."

The call ended, and Weston let out a long breath, relieved that Henry didn't seem to be too upset with him. In any case, Henry was right. They could solve their differences with alcohol and food— which was good, because Weston didn't have very many good friends, so he'd like to keep Henry close.

Henry arrived ten minutes later, and Weston opened the door to see him carrying a six-pack and a bag of steaks. Weston had spent those ten minutes telling himself he was going to be cool, totally cool, and he would not try to encourage Henry into having a long talk about their feelings.

"Are we okay?" Weston fretted.

Henry glanced skyward, sighing. "You're such a girl," he muttered, pushing past Weston to go inside.

Weston was pretty sure that meant he was forgiven.

"And before you say anything else," Henry continued, "Aiko talked to me, and fine, the mug thing was rude."

"Oh, good." Weston beamed. "Because I'm going on a date with Sidney tonight."

The six-pack of beer made an uncomfortably loud *clank* as it hit the kitchen counter. Henry turned, slowly, to stare at him. "Did I just hear you right? You called me over because you're having a *date* with the Leech?"

Ah, yes, Weston supposed Henry might not be too enthusiastic about that. "Exactly right," he confirmed. He was coming close to wringing his hands, so he stuffed them in his pockets instead.

"That's sudden," Henry remarked. He seemed to have gotten over his shock and was rustling around the kitchen instead, finding Weston's pans. "Do I have to call him by his real name now?"

"Only to his face," Weston allowed.

"Good, because I'm still not sure I even like the guy." Henry gave Weston a baffled stare as he unpacked the steaks. "Why the fuck are you going on a date with him? A week ago you hated him too."

A week ago Weston had still been utterly paranoid that he'd lose his job just because Sidney had been hired. He'd since been reassured, but he supposed Henry hadn't. "Because he's hot and brave and heroic and totally not selfish and—"

"You sound like you're describing some ridiculous fucking hero from your writing," Henry said, giving Weston a frown.

Weston smiled dreamily. "That's because he's just like that." He was as hot as Sentry, as passionate as Saunders, as courageous as Starson.

Henry clearly gave up. He groaned and turned to focus on the steaks. Weston moved into the kitchen with him, popping the caps off two bottles of beer and handing one to Henry. Soon, the smell of cooking meat filled the kitchen, abruptly reminding Weston that he hadn't had a very decent lunch.

A baseball game played on the television, which they watched as Henry cooked, occasionally commenting on the score. Weston's team was losing horribly, but he'd never been all that involved in baseball, so it was just an idle amusement to pass the time.

Henry dished up the steaks, and they retreated to Weston's couch. His laptop was open on the coffee table; Henry leaned forward, peering at it. "Science fiction?"

"Attempted science fiction," Weston corrected. "I keep having these crazily vivid dreams with great ideas, but I can never write them down."

Henry smirked a little. "Because you psych yourself out, man. You just want to have already written something. Starting's the hard part."

Weston gave Henry a grumpy frown. "And when did you become a writing guru?"

"Aiko writes sometimes." Henry shrugged. "Nothing serious, she says, but it's a hobby of hers."

Trying to figure out why Henry would know this about Aiko, Weston started cutting into his steak. Though he might be friends with Henry and decently friendly workmates with Aiko, he knew Henry and Aiko weren't good friends. Then again, they had become partners in crime on that stupid mug prank.

"Oh my fucking God, you're dating her," Weston yelped, turning a horrified stare on Henry.

Henry looked like a deer in headlights. "How... *how* did you figure that out?"

Weston pointed an accusing finger at him. "You teamed up with that stupid mug thing, and now you know that she writes!"

"Jesus." Henry got over his shock and started grinning. "Wow, Weston. The one time your paranoia is actually right."

"I should say congratulations, but you two dating is kind of like my siblings dating," Weston groaned. "And you're way too good for each other. You think that sarcasm is an accepted form of socialization."

"It's definitely not the lowest form of wit," Henry said, but he was glancing at Weston out of the corner of his eye.

Weston supposed he'd give Henry what he wanted. "Fine, congratulations," he finally said. "I still think it's weird, but if you like her, then go ahead."

"Oh, good, I've got your permission," Henry said dryly. "Now can you remind me why you're going on a date with the Leech again?"

"Because of all the reasons listed earlier. And I need you to help me pick what I wear," Weston admitted. "I pulled out my whole closet and I can't decide."

"And you think I'll have a better idea?" Henry looked at what Weston was currently wearing—jeans and a T-shirt with a picture of a band on it. "Okay, maybe I will. You can't dress yourself at all."

"That's what everybody tells me." Weston glanced down at his T-shirt. He liked that band—he couldn't see what was wrong with it.

"I thought gay men were supposed to be good at dressing themselves," Henry remarked. "You spend so much time in the closet, after all."

Weston couldn't help but laugh. He threw a couch cushion at Henry, who ducked it, laughing as well. "Okay, at least you're going on a date," Henry continued, begrudgingly congratulatory. "Look at us, having dates. Soon we'll have to give up our bachelor pads entirely."

"Perish the thought." Weston shuddered. He'd never been with someone long enough to move in with them; perhaps that was a good thing, considering his habits. He wasn't sure how somebody would put up with his midnight writing and caffeine benders, let alone his hatred of doing the laundry and washing the dishes.

When they finished their steaks, Weston led a reluctant Henry into his bedroom so that Henry could despondently shake his head at the pile of clothing on the bed. Weston didn't have very many *good* clothes, so after trying on four or five different combinations, he finally wound up in vaguely decent jeans, a nice shirt, and a blazer, the latter of which he hadn't even been aware that he owned.

After shooing Henry out so he could stare at himself in the mirror and wish he'd been born with a better face, Weston tried to do something with his hair. He'd been cursed with his father's hair: constantly unruly, a color between blond and brown with an irritating half wave to it. People kept telling Weston he could straighten his hair, but that seemed like far too much effort, especially since he could barely manage to shave every morning.

He eventually just ran his hands through it and declared it done. He'd need a haircut soon anyway. It was getting below his ears, and

Judy kept remarking that he looked as though he was trying to audition for a boy band.

"Okay, I think I look vaguely presentable," Weston announced as he walked out of the bathroom to meet Henry in the kitchen. The man had started on his second bottle of beer, which he held out to Weston.

"Drink. You're going to need it."

Weston wrinkled his nose. "I don't need to drink. Why would I need to drink?"

"Because when you get a few in you, you stop flapping around so much and actually resemble a normal human being," Henry replied. "Drink."

Reluctantly, Weston took the beer and had a few mouthfuls. He hadn't been on a date in some time; maybe some liquid courage was a good idea. He growled at Henry's attempts to tip the bottle up farther while he was drinking. "I'm not going *drunk*," Weston protested. "That would make me look like a lush."

"You can be a bit of a lush sometimes," Henry pointed out.

"Not *all* the time, though, so I'm not an alcoholic at all!" Weston said, feeling quite triumphant about that one. "And I will go to this sane and sober."

SANE might not have been the best word to use.

The first mistake of the night was when Weston said, "Here's your ass," instead of "Here's your glass." He'd been staring at Sidney's ass as they'd waited at the bar.

The second was accidentally spilling his drink all over Sidney's pants.

And the third was running into one of Weston's ex-boyfriends, Derek. Well, that last one wasn't actually Weston's fault. How was he to know Derek had decided to come to the same bar on the same night?

Since Derek was the kind of man who could never leave well enough alone, as soon as he spotted Weston, he approached and sat in the chair next to him. "Westie!"

"Please don't call me Westie." Weston cringed. "Didn't we agree on that?"

"I would never agree to that," Derek replied cheerfully.

"It makes me sound like a breed of dog."

Sidney very politely cleared his throat.

"Oh, shit, you've got company." Derek leaned over the table, offering his hand. "Derek Hunter. Are you the date?"

Weston groaned and buried his face in his hands. To his credit, Sidney just said, "I am. Sidney Romero."

Sidney, Weston noticed all over again, looked amazing in a dark-blue shirt that brought out the golden hues in his skin, and dark trousers. Weston had been idly fantasizing all night. He'd also been itching for a pencil to draw him, but dismissed the urge as soon as it appeared—for years, the only art he'd done was for work. He wasn't sure Sidney would appreciate a portrait in the style of an animal mascot.

"Derek, please go away," Weston said weakly. He and Derek had remained on good terms after their split; they'd only been together for two months, and they'd both admitted that they weren't very good for each other.

"Hell no, I'm enjoying this too much." Derek's grin was broad, and Weston saw Sidney smirk a little too. "Is this a first date? If it is, Sidney, I'm going to have to warn you off this one."

"It is the first date, but I'm quite attached to the idea of it." Sidney watched Derek over the rim of his glass as he took a sip. "I'm not sure there's much you could say to warn me off."

Derek raised his eyebrows. "Not even—"

"Not even." Sidney's voice was firm. Weston felt hope stir in his chest. Like the gallant knights of old, Sidney appeared to be protecting him. Weston could just imagine him in a shining suit of amour, a gleaming sword at his side. Not that Weston was exactly a fair maiden in distress, but he appreciated the image nonetheless.

Derek looked grudgingly impressed. "All right, I guess I'll leave you to do your date." Just as Weston began to think it was safe, Derek pinched his cheek with a grin. "Behave, Westie. Try not to break into hysterics around this one. He seems good for you."

Weston quietly resisted the urge to beat his head against the table as Derek left to go back to a group of friends. Sidney gently patted Weston's hand. "It's okay. I don't think your hysterics are that bad."

Despite himself, Weston started laughing. "Thank you?"

"You're welcome." Sidney gave him a brilliant smile.

"So, I'm told I'm really bad at first dates." Weston felt the need to apologize. "I honestly have no clue what to talk about. And by saying that out loud, I've revealed myself as even more awkward than I should let on."

"I anticipated that." Sidney's smile was small, but genuinely amused. He reached into his pocket and drew out a small stack of cardboard squares, held together by a rubber band. "I prepared these for you."

Weston took them as they were offered, and squinted down at them in confusion. He took the rubber band off and shuffled through them, his confusion only growing. They were printed with phrases like *First job that you utterly hated* and *What kind of pets do you like?*

"Did you just give me conversational topic flash cards?"

"I did." Sidney looked as though he was fighting the urge to laugh. "Please don't take it as a mocking gesture. I just noticed that you feel uncomfortable when you don't know if you have a set topic, so I thought these may help."

Far from feeling insulted, Weston stared down at the cards in awe. "These are fantastic!" He'd often been told that he suffered from the writer's plight of wishing there was a script for his own conversations. But now he had questions that would let him get to know Sidney even more, all without the struggle for an appropriate topic. "Okay, let's try these out."

He shuffled through them as Sidney sat with a patiently entertained expression, and stopped on one. "This one says, 'What are your parents like?'."

"That's an easy one." Sidney grinned at him. "I was raised by my father in Detroit. He was a woodworker."

Weston wanted to ask why Sidney's mother hadn't been in the picture, but perhaps that question was a bit too heavy for a first date, so instead he asked, "Yeah? What did he make?"

"Furniture at first." Sidney took a drink. "But when he got too arthritic for that, he started his own woodworking business." His smile made a turn for the rueful. "It went well at first, but it didn't last more than three years. That was what made me want to help small businesses."

That certainly explained a lot. Weston looked at Sidney with a new sort of admiration. No wonder people sometimes thought he came off as harsh or too invested—he *was* invested, out of a deep love of a small business and the want to see it succeed.

It reminded Weston of Saunders, how his zeal for his job made him come off as self-righteous and pedantic. And of Starson, his compassion for small colonies and the want to help them.

"I have absolutely no doubt that Sanderson Designs will be better off because of you," Weston told him. "As for me, both of my parents are currently retired in California, living the good life."

"Now I'm jealous," Sidney laughed. "What did they do?"

"My father was a hairdresser, my mother worked on Wall Street. Odd combination, I know, but they made it work. My sister is a physicist; she's in London at the moment." Which reminded Weston—he really should call her. "She's working on... I don't even know. Something about particles and antimatter."

"I'd be confused too." Sidney shook his head, bemused. "That's far too intellectual for me."

"Don't sell yourself short," Weston encouraged him. "She might do all that crazy smart shit, but she couldn't tell you the first thing about how a business works, not like you could."

"Too true," Sidney said, raising his glass.

"Next question?" Weston flipped through the cards again before settling on one. "Is this weird? It feels like I'm interviewing you."

"Isn't that what first dates practically are?" Sidney smirked.

Weston supposed that was true. "Okay, what kind of pets do you like?"

"Cats, definitely. They're self-reliant and they're good for people who work," Sidney replied. "I used to have one back in college. Well, I sort of had one—he was the campus cat that got ridiculously fat because we all doted on him."

Weston heaved an overdramatic sigh. "I guess we just won't work out, then," he said. "Because I'm a dog person. I'm sorry, Sidney. We'll just have to go our separate ways."

"Our first date was doomed from the beginning," Sidney agreed with a laugh. "Will you still remember me fondly?"

"Every day," Weston assured. "With my loyal dog by my side."

"Maybe we can compromise and get one of each?"

"If that's the problem-solving direction we're going, we'll end up with a house half modern and half shitty pseudo antique," Weston pointed out.

Sidney grinned widely. "That's okay, as long as your 'antiques' don't end up on my side of the house."

"Camel lamps are *art*," Weston insisted. "And I'm never parting with my geese rug."

Sidney made a noise that was half a laugh, half a groan. "Dear God, Weston. Are you a secret eccentric?"

"Only if 'secret eccentric' means that I have a highly evolved sense of beauty that most people are lacking." Sidney was still looking bemusedly pained, so on a whim, Weston leaned over the table to kiss him. They were in public, so it was only quick and incredibly chaste, but it made Weston smile broadly as he drew back. "You'll learn to appreciate corded phones that look like bananas, I promise you."

Sidney was touching two fingers to his lips, looking vaguely dumbfounded. Weston figured he might not be used to public displays of affection. "I'm sure I will," he said. Or maybe Sidney was startled at being kissed so suddenly on the first date. Weston had no clue; he'd been told that he should pay more attention to common dating rules.

"Next question!" Weston announced cheerfully, looking down at his flash cards again. Sidney really was a genius for thinking of these. "Worst birthday party ever?"

"Oh, God," Sidney chuckled. "That would be when I was nine. It wasn't bad, but my father would tell you it was. I apparently decided that inviting my whole class over would be a great idea. My poor father had to deal with twenty small children hopped up on sugar."

Weston frowned contemplatively. "I'm just trying to imagine you high on sugar." He squinted at Sidney. "Nope, can't see it."

"Well, I was smaller then," Sidney said dryly.

"Really?" Weston pulled an exaggerated expression of surprise. "And here I was thinking you'd popped out of an egg, fully formed. My worst birthday was probably my fifteenth. My parents took us skiing, and I somehow managed to stab myself in the face with my own skis."

Sidney raised his eyebrows, looking concerned—which Weston thought was adorable, considering it had been a very long time ago. "Were you badly injured?"

"No, I just broke my nose and got a big cut." Weston shrugged. "So I spent the majority of that birthday in the hospital. My parents were petrified at the time, but now that story gets brought out at parties as a funny story. Which, by the way, you are *never* allowed to ask for funny childhood stories from my parents."

"So there might be a possibility of meeting your parents?" Sidney smiled. It was half a sly expression, half hopeful.

"If you can deal with my pheasant mattress, then yes." Weston couldn't keep the same look of hope off his own face. "I'd really like that. I guess that means we'll also be having another date, which is good, because I feel like this one is going really well." He paused. "Crap. Henry made me promise I wouldn't ask for status updates on the date. Ignore that."

Sidney just laughed lowly. "I think it's going well too."

"That may be in part due to your flash cards," Weston admitted. "Normally I really do just sit and blurt out whatever crosses my mind, which gets awkward."

"I wouldn't mind." Sidney looked at him fondly, reaching across the table to take Weston's hand. "I like you. That means all of you. Even the parts of you that everybody says are strange."

The smile Weston felt on his lips was probably stupid looking, but he didn't care. He turned his hand over, palm to palm with Sidney's, so that he could link their fingers together. He didn't feel awkward or anxious, just content to be here with the man sitting opposite him. "I'm glad," he murmured. "I really like you too. Despite how third grade that sounds."

Maybe he should tell Sidney about all the dreams he'd had. Then again, when Weston tried to imagine someone telling that to him, it sounded kind of creepy. He wasn't sure how to frame it in a *my creative brain obsesses over you* kind of way.

On second thought, maybe he'd leave that out of future conversations with Sidney.

The rest of the date seemed to pass in a blur of good wine and better company. Weston was sure he'd never had a conversation that flowed so naturally; he wasn't entirely sure what to do with himself and the easy way with which he spoke around Sidney.

It somehow wasn't even awkward when Weston offered to drive Sidney home. On previous dates with other people, he had been well aware that saying so could be taken as a subtle suggestion that he was bored and wanted to get away from their company. Not this time—though perhaps Weston had been feeling less paranoid because he'd been enjoying himself.

As they drove, Sidney insisted on turning the radio to the local classic rock station. Weston pretended to grimace as Journey started playing.

"Seriously? Journey?" Weston shook his head, putting on a pitying look. "Can you even name one song other than that one everyone sings?"

"No. But it doesn't matter, because that song is the best," Sidney said. "Be thankful I don't torture you by singing it." With that, he gleefully turned the volume higher.

Weston couldn't even pretend to suffer silently; watching Sidney have fun was one of the most captivating sights Weston had ever seen. Gone was the reserved nature of Sidney's expressions, gone were the carefully guarded words. As he drove, he watched Sidney out of the corner of his eye and smiled to himself as Sidney bobbed his head in time to the music.

He pulled to a stop outside Sidney's place. "Your chariot has arrived, sir," he said grandly.

"I thought you're only supposed to say that when someone is *waiting* for a chariot," Sidney teased.

Weston shrugged. "It's still a chariot and it's still arrived, just with you inside it. It's valid."

He could hear Sidney laughing as they got out of the car. Weston hurried around the side of the car to catch up with Sidney so he could walk him to his door. He was a little nervous, not that he'd admit it out loud. Usually this was the part where Weston felt the need to make some awkward joke to relieve his own tension, except he just wound up *making* things awkward.

"I really enjoyed myself tonight," Sidney said. The curve of his lips held a small smile, something private and just for the two of them.

"Me too!" Weston blurted. "I definitely considered it a success."

Oh, God. Really? He definitely considered it a success? He sounded like he was discussing the latest mascot suit design with a client.

"Weston." Sidney sounded gently amused. "You can relax. It's just me. I'm not going to bite your head off."

Weston could point out that he was nervous for reasons other than potential decapitation by biting, but he decided not to. "Sorry," he said. "I'm told I'm a little awkward about things like this."

He was thankfully interrupted from more babbling when Sidney hooked his fingers under Weston's chin. And then, for a long few moments, Weston couldn't think about anything other than the deep brown of Sidney's eyes and the sharp slope of his cheekbones.

Sidney's lips then pressed against his.

It was only the most chaste of kisses, a brief contact before Sidney pulled away again. But Weston felt dazed, a little giddy from it, and he smiled stupidly at Sidney.

"Good night," Sidney murmured. He withdrew his hand, his fingertips trailing softly over Weston's jaw.

"Um. Good night." It wasn't the most suave of statements to reply with. "I'll see you at work tomorrow."

WESTON felt as though he was on cloud nine as he closed his apartment door behind him.

They'd shared a moment, a glorious moment, of doing nothing but looking at each other, and Weston couldn't remember the last time he'd been content to do that. Normally, just staring at someone bored him completely.

The kiss hadn't been as passionate as Wirrex's kiss with Starson, but Weston didn't mind. After all, he and Sidney had hardly been in a life-or-death situation.

He was light on his feet as he made his way to his laptop, still smiling to himself. As far as dates went, Weston would consider that one perfect. He hadn't felt like his usual awkward self, and Sidney was clearly comfortable enough in his company to open up, his expressions free of the reservation that normally tempered them.

Weston gave the laptop a glance but found himself looking past it to the notepad sitting next to it. He'd been writing a shopping list. Suddenly, he itched to pick it up and draw. He didn't give himself a chance to think too hard about it and psych himself out—Weston just picked up the notepad and pen and started sketching.

His fingers guided the pen through the smooth slopes of the ship *Nova*, the sleek wings and the gracefully angled stern. The image was so clear in his head that Weston couldn't stop, even when he made a mistake in the line of the engine. Ballpoint pen wasn't normally his chosen medium, but it didn't matter. What was more important was adding in the details, the heavyset printed letters of the ship's name, the registered date of creation underneath it.

He didn't notice half an hour passing by. The only thing that put a stop to his drawing was a slight cramp in his hand because of the narrow pen, and when Weston stopped, he stared down at the drawing.

It wasn't great. Honestly, it wasn't even all that good, Weston knew, and he was managing to be somewhat objective.

But he'd *drawn*.

Maybe Henry was right, in a way. Not just about his writing but about his art too. He psyched himself out, made himself so nervous about it that he couldn't even start. But after a date of easy companionship where Weston hadn't felt awkward at all, that same confidence translated to his art.

Weston dug his phone out of his pocket and snapped a picture of the sketch. He sent it to Sidney.

A minute later, he received a reply. *That's amazing! I knew you'd be a good artist. Now just keep practicing, and you'll get your inspiration back in no time.*

Weston grinned down at his phone. A second text popped up, again from Sidney: *You should meet my friends. How about this weekend?*

Weston didn't have to think too hard about his reply: *Looking forward to it.*

# Chapter
# Ten

"YOU'RE going to make him dinner?"

Weston nodded excitedly. "I am. I haven't decided what yet. And, okay, I haven't even asked if he wants me to make him dinner, but I'm going to ask later today. And hopefully he'll even say yes."

Henry stared at him. "But you're *you*. You don't make dinner. You have a half hour flappy-hands routine of"—Henry mockingly raised the pitch of his voice—"What do I do, should I make this, what if I make it wrong, what if I burn it, what if I get food poisoning and die, but that's not how *Martha* would make it."

"I'm not that bad," Weston protested.

"You *are* that bad. You do that dance and then you give up and order takeout, and that is why you're growing a stomach," Henry said.

"I am not growing a stomach!" Weston only barely managed to not shriek. He leaned over his desk to poke his finger against Henry's stomach. "And like you can talk!"

Henry batted his hand away. "At least I cook. What do you think you're going to make?"

"Lasagna." Weston sniffed. "I'm perfectly capable of that." Except he didn't know which recipe he was going to use. Did Sidney prefer simple lasagnas, or the really complicated ones that took four hours to cook? He wasn't a vegetarian, so meat would be okay, but what if he didn't even like lasagna?

"You're doing it right now."

"Shut up, I am not." Weston fidgeted with his tablet. Henry had dressed particularly smartly today; Weston assumed it was for Aiko's benefit. He'd seem them earlier, and they'd been disgustingly affectionate, holding hands as they'd walked in the door to work. Good for them. He just hoped that they never asked him and Sidney on a double date.

"Just don't burn your house down," Henry advised. "The Leech isn't worth *that* much."

Personally, Weston thought that Sidney was worth at least a few houses, but he wasn't going to say that to Henry's retreating back. "And don't forget there's a meeting at eleven!"

Weston glanced at his calendar, startled. He'd completely forgotten about that. They didn't often have company meetings, with Sanderson being so lax about things—but considering what Sanderson had told Sidney about the job cuts, perhaps it was about time they *started* having business meetings.

He wasn't looking forward to this at all.

TO SAY that the business meeting didn't go well was a slight understatement.

Weston drifted back to his office in a daze and stared blankly at his computer screen. All of Sanderson Designs' employees had packed themselves into the big meeting room that was hardly ever used. Nobody had been nervous because with a business like theirs, with a boss like Sanderson, one could normally trust that one's job was safe.

Sanderson had announced he was offshoring the entire sewing department. Apparently he could employ four people in Manila for the cost of one person over here, and the extra work required to liaise with a department in a different country, Sanderson said, would not be too difficult.

The entire boardroom had been in shock. Henry, Weston recalled with an upsetting clarity, had glanced over at Weston, looking utterly betrayed by what their boss had announced. As well he should, Weston thought; as Henry was manager of the sewing department, his job might be one of the first ones to go.

It would also mean some aspects of his job would change. Seeing the prototypes would take a lot longer, as they'd need to be shipped over, which might incur even more expense for the customers. Weston wouldn't be able to go see the work in progress. He supposed he could ask for photographs, but that wouldn't be the same as seeing the thing in person.

Weston was not overly fond of change, so this new future in his job didn't exactly make him happy.

He was still brooding by the time Sidney came into his office. Simultaneously, they said:

"How about I cook dinner for you on Saturday?"

"Would you like to come to an art thing a friend told me about?"

They paused, and Weston gave a faint laugh. "Sorry. You go first."

Sidney glanced behind him and closed the door to Weston's office. "I was talking to a friend of mine, Brian, and he mentioned something vaguely artistic sounding that he was attending this weekend. Would you like to come with me?"

"And how about I cook you dinner afterward?" Weston said hopefully. "I can at least try. We could make a day of it." He desperately needed something to look forward to.

"That sounds excellent." Sidney smiled at him; Weston caught a trace of sympathy in the expression. "I'm sorry to hear about what Sanderson said."

"You weren't at the meeting."

"I may have been listening in through the door," Sidney said shiftily. "I did stop before I was tempted to do the old glass-against-the-wall trick, though."

Despite his mood, Weston couldn't help but grin. "You ninja."

"Next I'll be crawling through the air vents," Sidney agreed dryly. "Spying on the technicians to get back at them for spying on everybody else's computers."

"They spy on computers?" Weston shot a startled glance toward his own computer. He hardly did anything unprofessional on it, but the thought made him slightly paranoid nonetheless.

Sidney smirked. "Only if you give them permission. Or if they're extra sneaky. So, Saturday, then? Good, I'll pick you up at noon."

"Wait," Weston wailed. "What about the computer spies? You can't just insinuate I'm being spied on and then not give me more information!"

Sidney was still laughing even after he walked out into the hallway, leaving Weston staring dubiously at his computer. After a long moment of contemplation and telling himself he was probably being irrational, he stuck a piece of masking tape over the webcam. It wasn't as if he used it for anything.

WORK passed in an uneventful manner until Friday, which Weston was thankful for, but the tension in the air palpably rose every day. Every single one of the staff was waiting for the hammer to fall, and Sanderson hadn't announced when he was going to make the job cuts, only that he would make them at some point in the future.

Aiko had started talking about getting another job. Her shoulders had been slumped at their Thursday lunch, a far cry from her normally confident and forthright personality. She and Henry had been holding hands for nearly the entire time, and instead of wanting to tease them, Weston had only felt sympathy.

Still, the thought of a pleasant Saturday kept his own mood from plummeting to rock bottom, so he wasn't entirely depressed when he woke up late on Saturday morning. This time, Weston decided he could dress himself, as he'd only be wearing casual clothes—he had, however, been advised to give the band T-shirts a miss, which he took into consideration.

When noon rolled around, the doorbell rang.

"You're very punctual, Mr. Romero," Weston greeted as he opened the door. Sidney was dressed casually too, in a jacket and a striped scarf, though he somehow managed to look very sharply composed.

"I do try," Sidney replied, a smile in his eyes. "Shall we go?"

They should, but Weston wanted to do something else first. Namely, lean forward and wrap a hand around Sidney's elbow to tug him into a light kiss. He felt a tight band of nervousness within him ease as Sidney happily kissed back, one of his hands going to Weston's back.

"So what is this artistic thing you're taking me to?" Weston asked as they drew back. Perhaps kissing a man in public in his neighborhood wasn't the smartest thing to do, but he didn't care. Let everybody see.

"It's a poetry reading."

Weston blinked at Sidney. "A poetry reading." His first reaction was of disdain—he wasn't much of a poetry person, and from what he knew, poetry readings were for unwashed hippies and teenagers who self-expressed by wearing black. But, he had to remind himself, that wasn't fair. He should give it a go. "Okay. I've never been to one, but I'll try anything once."

The drive there was pleasant, with Sidney switching to the local classic rock channel and attempting to convert Weston to David Bowie. Weston was once again surprised to find himself mostly free of nerves. Something about Sidney just calmed him right down and made him feel like a normal human being who didn't overthink everything to death.

The event was on the other side of town, in a small café Weston had never been to. It seemed, from first glance, to be Scottish themed. Bemused, Weston glanced over the decor, the café sign—which bore a picture of bagpipes—the posters stuck to the outside of the building. There were pictures in the café window, long faded from years of being exposed to sunlight; and, oddly, a massive painting of a picture of french fries. Weston thought that might be a bit out of place, considering the rest of the theme.

Sidney got them a small table up against the inside wall, and they ordered coffee. A dozen people had already gathered, both sitting and standing. At the front of the café was a small stage where a desk had been set, a number of books stacked on top of it, and a sweater-vest-clad man nervously pushing his glasses up stood next to it. The event organizer, Weston presumed.

"Is there a theme for this?" Weston leaned over to murmur to Sidney, not wanting to break the quiet hush of the room. "Do we have to get up and read poetry?"

"Only if you want to," Sidney assured him. He waved to the man in the sweater-vest, who Weston assumed was Brian.

"I didn't exactly bring anything with me," Weston apologized. The idea of standing up in front of a bunch of people and reading poetry seemed horrifying to him, though, so he was glad he hadn't been told to prepare anything in advance, as he might have felt compelled to.

The first person—a woman in a skirt that dragged on the floor where she walked—stepped up to the table. "It's okay," Sidney said lowly in reply. "Still, if you do want to, Brian accepts impromptu poetry."

"Impromptu poetry?" Weston knew he should probably quiet down as the woman started reading, but he had to ask.

"You can just improvise," Sidney explained. "If you're really good at poetry."

"Oh." Weston had never heard of *improvising* poetry, but he supposed it could be done. He dimly noticed that the woman's poem seemed to be something about hats, but he wasn't really paying attention; he was more interested in studying Sidney, who looked rapt with anticipation.

"I dread to put it on," the woman intoned. "Its gaping crevice would envelop my head."

Weston couldn't stop the embarrassing snorting noise he made in reaction. He brought his hands up to cover his mouth, faking a cough.

"For I feel woe, at the concept of *un chapeau*."

Weston then desperately tried to stop the giggle that threatened to sound. Sidney looked at him, his expression stern, but there was a smile curving at the very corner of his lips, barely visible.

"I fear, I tremble, I am crushed by the cold anvil of cocklaphobia."

As Weston bit down on his fingers to suppress a laugh, his shoulders shook in silent amusement. Why was it that things were always so much funnier when he couldn't laugh out loud? Was cocklaphobia even a real word? He'd have to look that one up when he got home.

The poem about the fear of hats was mercifully short, and by the time the woman made her way back into the crowd, Weston's chest hurt from contained laughter.

"Oh my God," he muttered to Sidney. "Oh my *God*, Sidney."

"That was rather an odd start," Sidney replied, struggling to withhold his own amused smile.

"I think my life has been changed. No, seriously. I've been enlightened to the struggles of those who 'walk a lonely path without hats'."

Then again, Weston wasn't sure he could judge too hard. He wasn't the best writer himself; he was sure he hadn't quite gotten to the level of writing flowery poetry about headwear, though.

Sidney playfully hit him in the arm. "Don't be mean," he said, his eyes alight with humor. "Instead, answer me this: what are you making me for dinner tonight?"

As they waited for the next person to take the stage, Weston answered, "Lasagna. Hopefully."

"Hopefully?" Sidney cocked an eyebrow. "Have you never cooked it before?"

"I don't really cook often." Weston lifted one shoulder in a shrug, faintly embarrassed. "I know I should, but it freaks me out. I always start thinking about what would happen if I make it wrong."

Sidney leaned in close, his lips nearly brushing Weston's ear. "I could think of a few ways to relax you."

Since Weston wasn't often the recipient of innuendo, it took him a few seconds to get it. Then he grinned, turning his head slightly so that his and Sidney's lips were merely inches apart. "Oh, really? That's very forward of you."

"I'm told I'm forward when I'm really into someone."

Weston marveled at how different Sidney sounded to the personality he presented at work. Here, Sidney wasn't reserved or shy at all. He was a man who knew exactly what he wanted, and that was rather attractive.

"Lucky me," Weston murmured. The other conversations in the café had faded to his ears, unimportant and trivial compared to Sidney. All that existed was the depths of Sidney's eyes, the lighter flecks of hazel against dark brown, the mischievous little smile on his lips.

Weston didn't notice the next poet stepping up to the table until their moment was broken with a loudly proclaimed, "My soul bleeds like a stuck pig!"

The volume of the man's voice startled Sidney and Weston both, and they narrowly avoided knocking their foreheads together as they turned to look at the table.

"The machete of heartbreak has skewered me," the new poet continued woefully.

Weston couldn't speak. He was too busy burying his face against Sidney's shoulder, trying again not to laugh. He could feel Sidney shaking slightly with the same urge. Sidney moved his arm, wrapping it loosely around Weston's back, holding him close.

Even when the urge to laugh began to fade, Weston kept his head resting against Sidney's shoulder. He didn't want to move, so he turned just enough that he could continue watching the stage, pressed tightly against Sidney's side.

The new few speakers recited poems from considerably more famous poets, which were considerably easier on the ear. Weston noticed Sidney smiling at one in particular.

"Shakespeare's sonnet 130," Sidney murmured to Weston. "It's my favorite."

Weston had never been much of a Shakespeare fan—he realized the literary merit of the man, of course, but personally he'd never been able to get into his works. But he did know the sonnet the man at the table was reciting. "Yeah? Why's that?"

"It's a vision of love so rarely seen," Sidney replied. "He acknowledges her faults. He is aware that she's not some goddess of beauty and that no woman can actually look like the flowery descriptions he uses. He sees her faults and he loves her because of them, because she is special to him."

"You sound like you've studied this," Weston remarked, impressed.

"I took a few courses on English literature in college." Sidney grinned quickly at him.

"Really? Suddenly you're so much hotter," Weston said.

"As hot as white snow and red coral?"

"Hotter," Weston assured.

Sidney curled his fingers around Weston's, and they smiled at each other before turning back to listen to the poetry. Weston was surprised to find that he was thoroughly enjoying himself. He certainly hadn't expected to enjoy a poetry recital, but Sidney's company made it worthwhile.

Thankfully, the rest of the recited poetry was much the same, though Weston would admit to a new fondness of the terrible stuff that had been spoken at first. He could identify with being a bad writer but still having ideas he desperately wanted to write down, although he hadn't, as of yet, used any phrases like *machete of heartbreak*.

Once the event was over, Sidney introduced him to Brian. Brian was a friend Sidney had made at his last job, a mild-mannered man with a surprisingly sharp wit and a love of poetry that bordered on the obsessive. Weston promised to return for another event and was surprised to find that he actually meant it. It had been a somewhat strange outing, but it had been fun.

It was late afternoon by the time Sidney drove them back to Weston's house, and Weston wasted no time in finding the recipe for lasagna. He'd shopped earlier, making sure he had all the ingredients, and it didn't look *too* hard to make.

"If this starts to be a regular thing, I have no idea how I'm going to keep my shape," Sidney joked as they cut vegetables for a side salad. Weston had tried to get Sidney to sit down, but the man had insisted on helping. "I'm going to need to fit in a few extra hours of working out every week."

Weston found his thoughts going to Sentry. Though he was aware Sentry was a dream character in a high fantasy setting, he had to imagine that the dragon's physique was much like Sidney's—he imagined that because Sentry had been hot, and he'd quite like it if Sidney had the same body. "You'll be fine," he replied.

"Seriously, I have a crap metabolism," Sidney said. He hooked his fingers under the bottom of his shirt and lifted it to sigh at his stomach. "See? Every morning I work out and I don't even have abs."

Weston happily did as he was told and looked. He was startled to find that Sidney's lower torso was not like Sentry's at all. Where Sentry had had clearly defined muscles and an incredible six-pack, Sidney's stomach was flat with only a bare amount of definition.

He tried not to feel disappointed. "You look perfectly in shape," Weston attempted to assure Sidney.

Sidney just frowned again and let his shirt drop. They fell into silence as they continued cooking, the clatter of utensils and the television in the background the only noise in the room. Though Weston wasn't a good cook, he was deft enough with a knife, and it didn't take them long to get the lasagna in the oven.

The day before, Weston had nearly made himself sick with indecision over how to present the food. He couldn't make up his mind about whether he should go casual, and they would eat on the couches; or if he would go romantic, and eat at the table. He'd eventually decided on the latter option, so while Sidney watched over the lasagna, Weston got the table ready. It was only a small one, square with four seats, but he hoped it would do.

Weston tried to figure out if a candle was too much. He had one lying around somewhere from an earlier attempt at a romantic dinner a year ago, but seeing as that date had failed, he decided not to jinx this one by bringing the candle out. Maybe it was bad luck.

After ushering Sidney to the table, Weston served up the lasagna with a side of salad and poured some red wine to go along with it. "I hope it's okay," he said. "It looks okay, but looks can be deceiving."

Sidney took a bite and chewed thoughtfully. A smile spread over his face. "It's good, Weston," he assured him. "We succeeded. I think that calls for congratulations."

Weston grinned, holding his wine glass up to tap it against Sidney's. "Go us," he said happily. "I'm pretty sure it's only edible because you helped."

"I think you do yourself a disservice," Sidney replied, reaching over the table to tuck an errant curl behind Weston's ear. The action made Weston smile stupidly. "It's perfectly good."

Since Weston had often been told that constantly insisting he was crap at everything got boring for everybody within hearing range, he went with a more graceful "Thank you. And thank you for inviting me out. I really enjoyed today."

"Me too." Sidney looked perfectly content, and Weston felt much the same way.

"So." He looked hopefully at Sidney. "More dates?"

Sidney grinned widely. "Definitely more dates."

WESTON barely felt human when he trudged into work on Monday.

It was his own fault, he knew. He'd been up all night, his thoughts going in circles much like they had on Saturday night. He'd attempted to write some but hadn't gotten very far; his own thoughts had been too distracting.

It all came down to Sidney's torso. That was where the thoughts had started. Weston was well aware that it was a completely irrational base for his circular thoughts, but as circular thoughts were so rarely rational, he decided not to worry about it too much. It was Sidney's stomach. Decent for a man of his age, really.

But not the glistening, rippling abdomen of Weston's dreams.

Like any small child, he'd once made a list of the particular characteristics he'd like to find in his soul mate. He still had it floating around his apartment in an old box somewhere, and Weston clearly remembered what the list said: good-looking, brave, smart, funny, rich, likes jelly beans.

Sidney did indeed match some of those criteria, and Weston felt he could let the last requirement slide. Sidney was good-looking, and he was smart, and he was definitely funny once he felt comfortable enough around somebody to open up. He wasn't rich, but Weston had hardly been expecting that.

But like so many dreams, those characteristics had been in the extreme. Good-looking didn't just mean pleasing to the eye, it meant *stunningly* good-looking. So outrageously handsome that men and women everywhere fell over themselves just to get a look at that ridiculously attractive person. Smart didn't just mean sensible, it meant a very rare kind of genius. And rich didn't just mean rich, it meant *wealthy*: cruising on million-dollar boats and sipping champagne from diamond glasses. Brave meant taking on dragons and great evils, not merely standing up for one's opinions. Though Weston had long since accepted that he would never date the hottest, smartest, richest, bravest man on the planet, he still couldn't help comparing Sidney to Sentry, Saunders, and Starson.

And God, he felt guilty for doing it.

It wasn't fair to Sidney, Weston knew. They were figments, dream images. Ideals that so few people in reality actually achieved.

He'd been staring blankly at his computer for the last few minutes, so Weston shook his head sharply to get his thoughts under control and dug his knuckles into his temple. He was exhausted from so little sleep, but he still had to work.

He was halfway through an e-mail when Sidney arrived. Unlike his usual entrances, Sidney looked tense. "Check your e-mail," he said.

"Morning," Weston greeted, waving at the seat. Despite his earlier thoughts, he still smiled at Sidney's arrival, feeling that warmth of fondness wash over him. So what if Sidney didn't have Sentry's abs? He still liked Sidney. "I was just writing one, actually. What's so important?"

Sidney didn't reply, so Weston clicked through his e-mail and opened the one that had recently arrived. It was from Sanderson. He read it, his mood growing sourer by the second.

"Shit," Weston said.

"I know," Sidney murmured. He looked worried now.

"He's... shit, he's doing the job cuts today." Weston transferred his dumbfounded stare from the monitor to Sidney. "I didn't expect it to happen this quick."

"Neither did I." Sidney grimaced. He reached across the desk, then took Weston's hand, and gripped it tight. "I don't know what's going to happen, Weston. But before those meetings happen, I want you to know that I didn't make any of those decisions."

"I know," Weston assured him. "Of course I know." He gave a faint laugh. "Funny. I used to think *you* were the villain in this, back when you first got here. I was so paranoid. Now I know who the real villain is."

It was Sanderson. The man who had once practically embodied the ideals of small business, now turned to greedy profit.

"Weston," Sidney said lowly, squeezing his hand, "there's no *villain* here. This isn't about good and evil. It's just business. Unfortunate business, yes, but just business all the same."

"But you talked to him, right?" Weston raised hopeful eyes to meet Sidney's gaze. "You said you'd try to do whatever you could to save this place."

Sidney exhaled slowly, frowning. "I tried. But I don't know how much use I was."

"I have faith in you." Weston smiled at him, thoughts of Starson circling in the back of his mind. Starson had saved an entire small colony; surely Sidney could save one small business. The former was just based on the latter, after all.

"I think your faith might be a bit misplaced," Sidney said ruefully. "But I did my best. We'll see how much that counts for."


WHEN Weston was summoned to Sanderson's office, he walked as slowly as he could, dreading the possibilities. In a few minutes, he might hear that his job had been cut. He had no idea how long it would take him to find another job, and he'd been working at

Sanderson Designs for so long that he wasn't sure how well his skills would translate into other jobs.

He entered the office. Sanderson looked a little like Santa Claus without the beard. A little portly and red-cheeked, Sanderson always had a smile on his face. He never failed to give words of encouragement when they were needed, and his employees all took inspiration from him, trusting that he would do the best for the company.

Sanderson wasn't smiling now.

"Good morning," Weston greeted him, attempting to sound confident and assured. He crossed the room to sit in one of the chairs in front of Sanderson's desk and folded his hands in his lap. "How are you, Mr. Sanderson?"

"Well enough, Weston." Sanderson looked tired. "I suppose you know why you're here."

"Yes, sir." Nervousness crept into Weston's voice. The office began to look somewhat ominous now. The sun slanted into the room to bounce off a metal paperweight, sending the reflection right into Weston's eye, seemingly perfectly tailored to discomfort him. The slow ticking of the clock was surely tuned louder in effort to make visitors on edge.

"I might as well get right down to business." Sanderson's expression became slightly more pleasant. "Your job is being kept, Weston."

"Oh, thank God," Weston blurted, sagging in his seat. "Thank you, Mr. Sanderson." He felt as though a massive weight had just lifted off his shoulders, and he laughed giddily. "Seriously, thank you."

Sanderson smiled at him, looking more like the boss everybody knew and loved. But although Weston had been spared, other people would not be.

"Can I ask why you're doing this?" Weston had to ask. He normally strived to be polite and unobtrusive with his higher-ups, but curiosity was nagging at his mind. "It's just, none of us expected a move like this."

"Business, Weston," Sanderson replied. "The circle of life. The bigger businesses do well, the smaller businesses do less well."

Weston didn't find that to be a particularly satisfying answer, but seeing as he was hardly going to sit around and debate small business with his boss, he merely nodded. "Thank you, Mr. Sanderson."

Sanderson waved him off and Weston left the office considerably less cheery than he suspected he should feel, having just been told he could continue working in the near future. Their boss had changed. He was no longer the optimistic man who was proud of the business he'd fought for.

Weston didn't want to think the word *sellout*, but it was there in his thoughts nonetheless. He knew it wasn't fair to Sanderson. Maybe Weston had it wrong; maybe Sanderson was just doing the only thing he could to keep his business afloat. But with the extremely high possibility that some of his friends' jobs might be cut, Weston couldn't feel very charitable and understanding right then.

Weston couldn't immediately see Sidney anywhere on his walk back to the office. He presumed he was actually doing something productive, unlike Weston, who was going to be getting a congratulatory coffee and maybe a slice of that cake Judy had brought in last Friday. He felt he deserved it.

# Chapter Eleven

"I DON'T have a fucking job."

Henry was currently facedown on the bar counter, his shoulders slumped. If he slouched any farther, he would fall off the barstool.

"Weston. *Weston.* I don't have a fucking job."

Henry was also completely shit-faced.

Weston rubbed his back. "I know," he said, sympathetic. "I'm so sorry."

"The entire fucking sewing department. Offshored," Henry muttered. "To fucking *Manila.*"

"You're using the word fuck a lot," Weston interjected helpfully.

"It makes me feel better."

"Completely understandable."

It was strange, being torn between relief over his own situation and upset at Henry's. Weston wanted to celebrate, but he didn't want Henry to think he was rubbing it in his face.

He hadn't seen Sidney for the rest of the day, except for a brief encounter in the hallway where Sidney had hugged him, told him he was happy for him that he was keeping his job, and apologized that he was going to be really busy. At that time, Weston hadn't heard the news about Henry and the rest of the sewing department.

Sidney had said he'd try to help. Weston didn't know exactly what Sidney had done, but the result was clear: the sewing department was gone. Sidney hadn't managed to do anything, and Weston tried to not feel disappointed. He tried to not make comparisons to Starson, the savior of a small colony. He tried, because Weston knew Starson wasn't real. Starson was just a dream, albeit a dream character who was similar to Sidney.

But he couldn't help thinking Starson would have saved them. Those courageous men, that stereotypical protagonist figure that Weston had grown up reading about—they were heroes. They stopped at nothing. They self-sacrificed; they did whatever they could to achieve their goal.

Weston stared hard at the rows of bottles behind the bar, willing himself to stop digging deeper into that line of thought. His rational mind—though it might not make many appearances in his day-to-day life—told him that placing such expectations on Sidney was ridiculous. His emotional mind, however, spoke differently. That mind made him disappointed that Sidney wasn't a storybook hero, a rugged action movie star, a quick-witted theater character.

Sidney was just a man. A flawed man who hadn't been able to help as much as he wanted to.

"Shit, at least I can maybe stay at Aiko's, right?" Henry said dejectedly.

"You can sleep on my couch too. The offer's open," Weston told him.

Henry raised a disbelieving eyebrow at him. "Let's see. My hot girlfriend's bed or your couch?"

"My couch is awesome," Weston said defensively. "It folds out and everything." Sobering, he continued, "But seriously, Henry. If you do wind up needing a place to stay, my place is yours."

"Thanks." Henry ordered another beer for them both, waving a hand at the bartender. "I mean it."

"I know." Weston slung an arm around his shoulders, feeling overly friendly with a bit too much alcohol in him. "I'm awesome too."

"But just so you know, if Sidney's sleeping at your place, I'm not even going near your couch."

Weston pulled a face at Henry. "I'm sure we'd keep our activities in the bed."

"I know you would, you're horrendously vanilla." Henry smirked. He kept speaking before Weston could protest. "But sound carries, man."

"True." Weston took a long drink of his beer. "He tried to help, you know. He said he was going to try to minimize damage."

"Really?" Henry looked surprised at that but then shook his head. "That's good of him."

Weston was near drunk, so he felt he could be excused for belatedly remarking, "Hey, you called him Sidney! Not the Leech."

Henry snorted. He didn't look so revolted at the mention of the productivity consultant, not like he normally did. "Yeah, well, if you're dating him, he can't be all that bad. You guys dating is actually a worse reflection on him. He must have low standards."

Weston elbowed Henry—carefully, so he didn't upset his drink. "Probably," he had to agree. "I'm not exactly the sharpest fish in the sea."

"You're mixing your metaphors."

"Not if we're talking about swordfish," Weston mused.

Henry, though he was clearly still upset over the loss of his job, laughed. "You're such an idiot," he said fondly, bumping his shoulder against Weston's. "But if the Leech really did try to talk to Sanderson, maybe I judged him wrong."

Weston brightened. "It would be really cool if you guys could be friends."

Not too long ago, Henry would have looked as though he were close to vomiting in his mouth from the very thought of it. Now, though, he nodded slowly. "Maybe that could happen. Shit, it wasn't *his* idea to offshore the sewing department."

"He looked really upset at the idea of it happening," Weston murmured. "He told me he's a productivity consultant because he's really invested in small businesses. His dad started one years ago, but it got crushed."

"Just like Sanderson Designs is getting." Henry's smirk was wry. He raised his beer and knocked it against Weston's. "To the big business bootheel, crushing the unfortunate."

"That's a morbid toast," Weston remarked, but he returned it nonetheless. "But it would be cool if you gave Sidney a chance. Maybe we could all have lunch together or something soon?"

"I'm just drunk enough to agree," Henry said.

"What a touching sentiment." Weston snorted. "'Hey Sidney, do you want to have lunch with Henry and me? He only agreed because he was drunk.'"

Henry shrugged. "Your love life is just something I want to steer clear of, Weston. It's not *who* it is. It's just that I have a fear that all you do in your date's company is make dumb cow eyes at them and ignore everything else. It sounds completely saccharine."

"That is so not true," Weston protested. "I do other things. Like... talk!"

Henry started laughing at him before he could think of any other things, so Weston gave up.

"So where do you think you'll go next?" he asked curiously. "Have you given it any thought?"

"Not really," Henry admitted. "I'll have to start looking for jobs tomorrow. Shit, I haven't done that in a while." He paused and then gave a huff of a laugh. "Maybe I'll give Gucci a call."

Weston grinned at him. "I'm sure they'd take you in a heartbeat, Henry."

They parted ways an hour later. Weston made sure Henry got himself into a cab, and got one himself and headed home.

Drinking wasn't exactly his usual motivation for writing, so he didn't attempt any that night. Instead, Weston got ready for bed and all but collapsed on it when he got there, groaning as the room spun around him. Five minutes later he remembered he should drink a glass of water, so Weston laboriously crawled out of bed before returning to slip between his sheets once more, his head falling heavily on his pillow.

He drifted into sleep and dreamed.

—+——+——+——+——+——+——+——+——+——+——+—

"Our engine seems to be ironically broken," Wentworth said and gazed out at the lonely dirt road their car had stopped upon. "Hey, look, it's the forest that's rumored to have all those ghosts in it! We should go!"

"Are you kidding?" Stephen stared at Wentworth as though he was stupid. Which he probably was. "You want to go alone, into a dark haunted forest, at night. Yes, that's a fantastic idea."

"It totally won't end with one or both of us getting killed at all," Wentworth said confidently.

The dream shifted, and the forest slipped away.

"Oh no, it's the Sharpshooter, the Scourge of the West, the Quick Draw!" someone in the saloon wailed. "It's Slim Redhand!"

Spurs clanked against the wooden floor. A tumbleweed drifted past.

Slim squinted into the darkness of the saloon, his weathered face enigmatic and mysterious. Winston cowered behind the bar.

Footsteps walked closer. "Whiskey," Slim rasped. Winston peered up over the bar, his heart beating like a drum. The cowboy was so handsome he felt like he could swoon. But no! He was an outlaw! Such a romance would be taboo yet thrilling, the topic of many stories to come!

—+——+——+——+——+——+——+——+——+——+——+—

Weston briefly woke up, utterly baffled over the contents of his dreams. He fell asleep once more.

—+——+——+——+——+——+——+——+——+——+——+—

"I'm half vampire, half werewolf, half kappa," Wade boasted. "Since vampires and werewolves are so overdone, I'm so unique because I picked something typically unattractive and lesser known."

"You can't be three halves," Saelig pointed out.

"Yes, I can," Wade shrieked. "Don't mock my uniqueness!"

The dreams bled together, mixed, and then separated.

Sewell smiled at him and took his hand. Wolfram grinned back. "I do."

They kissed.

Wolfram recited Shakespeare's sonnet 130.

Sewell was perfect to him. He wasn't a genius. He wasn't a sword-wielding hero. He wasn't model material.

He had terrible bedhead in the mornings. One of his eyebrows quirked upward more than the other. He was grumpy when things didn't go as planned. He had flaws. Lots of them.

And that was okay.

—▪——▪——▪——▪——▪——▪——▪——▪——▪——▪——▪——

THE next day, a quarter of Sanderson Designs' workforce didn't want to do much work. Weston understood that completely—they'd been given two months, and then they had to find new jobs. Weston didn't feel like doing much work either, but that was mostly because he was slightly hungover.

Still, he had a blue jay mascot suit to finish and Sidney to take out to lunch at midday, so he drank as much water as he could and tried to get himself feeling better so that he wasn't a complete waste of space by lunchtime.

Sidney met him at the building entrance, smiling when Weston grabbed him in a hug. He'd missed seeing Sidney yesterday, even though that seemed slightly ridiculous, seeing as he'd hardly been a very long time without him. Instead of going to a café, they went to get sandwiches and Weston took Sidney to a nearby park.

It seemed criminal to waste the good weather—bright and sunny, just a faint breeze—so they sat on a park bench overlooking the river, sandwiches in hand.

"I know I said it yesterday, but congratulations again on keeping your job," Sidney said, bumping his shoulder against Weston's.

"Thanks." Weston grinned back at him. "Although I'm not sure *congratulations* is the right word to use. I didn't exactly achieve anything; it was all Sanderson's choice."

"Still, I'm happy for you." Sidney reached out to take Weston's hand and gently tangled their fingers together, resting their joined hands on Weston's knee.

Weston leaned back against the bench, contentedly munching on his sandwich, absently rubbing his thumb over Sidney's knuckles. Sidney had an uncanny knack of being able to settle him, to make him feel as though he was on an even keel. It was practically a revelation; nobody else had managed to make him feel so at peace.

He occasionally threw bits of crust to the geese paddling nearby in the river, and tipped his face up to feel the warmth of the sunlight. Sidney broke the silence by saying, "I'm sorry I didn't manage to do more to save the sewing department."

Weston looked over at him, questioning. "It's not your fault."

"You asked me to save the company." Sidney smiled very faintly. "I tried. I talked to Sanderson, I tried to outline other options for him, but he didn't take any of them." He hesitated, squeezing Weston's hand. "And I know that it's not my fault. But I feel... I feel like you're disappointed."

Weston shook his head. "Sidney, come on. I didn't expect you to save the whole company."

Didn't he, though? He'd asked Sidney to do so. He'd been sure Sidney *would* be able to do so.

"I think you did," Sidney said gently. There was no judgment in his tone, which Weston was grateful for. "Which was why I felt the need to apologize." He looked sad. A slight frown touched the corner of his lips, emphasizing the guilty downward tilt to his eyebrows. He'd said he knew it wasn't his fault the sewing department had been cut, but he still looked guilty.

For a long few moments, Weston didn't understand. Why was Sidney feeling both things?

"I... shit. I'm sorry." Weston sighed, eyes downcast. "I guess I did think you'd be able to do it."

"Why is that?" Sidney's tone was still nonjudgmental. "I'm just one man."

It was time to come clean, Weston supposed. He just hoped it didn't make him sound like an extraordinarily creepy stalker.

"I've been having these dreams," he admitted. "Just bear with me, because I know that sounds weird up front. I keep having these amazing, vivid dreams that are like whole stories. There's plot and characterization, and character growth, and an entire world fleshed out. They're better ideas than I could ever come up with when I'm awake."

Sidney was still watching him, so Weston continued, "In the first dream I had, it was shortly after you started working here. I was this fantasy warrior type, and there was a dragon named Sentry. Everybody thought he was a monster, but he wasn't. The next one was like a detective story, and my partner, Saunders, was falsely accused of a crime. Then there was a science fiction one, where a guy named Starson saved as many as he could of a small colony of people that were about to be massacred."

It all sounded so stupid when he said it out loud, but Weston saw a dawning understanding on Sidney's face. "All three are names beginning with S," he murmured.

"And all of them looked like you too." Weston gave a rueful smile. "And they were you, in a sense. Sentry was falsely vilified. Saunders was wrongly accused. Those were back when I was paranoid about you; I thought you were going to bring the whole company down around us."

Sidney surprised him by laughing quietly. "I'm glad you think differently now."

"I do," Weston hastened to assure him. "I definitely know differently now. But you know me. I was paranoid and kind of crazy."

"*Was?*" Sidney smirked at him.

Weston punched him in the shoulder. "You're so horrible to me," he said fondly. "Anyway, there was the dream with Starson saving me, and... well. I guess it's pretty obvious what happened."

It was embarrassing to realize what he'd been doing. He'd dismissed Sidney as being average-looking just because he hadn't had the unrealistic body of a fantasy shape-shifter. He'd expected Sidney to save them because his dream counterpart had done so. And Weston was only just realizing that now.

"Fuck," he muttered, rubbing a hand through his hair. "I didn't even think about it, really. I just expected you to be like the dream."

His dreams, celebrity ideals, romance novel heroes. He'd based his expectations of Sidney on them, and when Sidney had failed to live up to Sentry, Saunders, and Starson, Weston had been disappointed.

Now he felt as though he might actually be the worst person alive.

"I didn't guess about the dreams." Sidney pressed in closer until their shoulders rested together, their knees lightly touching. "But I did pick up on the expectations. May I be honest, Weston?"

"Please do," Weston managed to say. He couldn't shake the feeling that Sidney was about to get extremely angry and yell at him.

That wasn't what happened, thankfully.

"It made me feel terrible that I didn't live up to your ideals," Sidney confessed softly.

"You did!" Weston instinctively tried to protest, wanting to make Sidney feel better.

"No, Weston, listen to me." Sidney gently tugged on his hand. "I know I didn't. I could see it in your eyes. You would look at me with such awe, such faith, and it made me feel like I could do anything. And when I failed, I could see that in your eyes too."

Weston had tried to hide the disappointment. He obviously hadn't been successful. "I am so fucking sorry," he said miserably. "I didn't mean to make you feel like shit. I guess I just spend so much time in my head that real people become a bit of a mystery to me."

"That might be it," Sidney said. Weston was relieved to see a smile on his lips; it made him feel slightly less like absolute scum. "I am rather flattered that you dreamed about me, though."

Weston laughed a little. "I think my subconscious was trying to tell me something with them. That you weren't the villain I thought you were, or that you were a really good guy."

"Did we do anything interesting in those dreams?"

"Uh." Weston was torn between embarrassment and amusement. "We kissed in the science fiction one. That was before we had our first date."

Instead of grinning like Weston expected him to, Sidney frowned slightly. "Did that… was that dream why you agreed to the date?"

It took Weston a second to parse the meaning of what he said—Sidney was asking if the dreams were the only reason that Weston was interested in him. "Oh, hell no," he said firmly. "I was interested before that. I mean, that might have given me the courage to accept, but trust me, I'm not going on dates with you just because of the dreams."

"Good." Sidney looked relieved. "I'm glad."

Weston still felt guilty, so he wanted to apologize again. "I really am sorry. I don't *really* expect you to be a hero or a major Casanova or anything. I just got so caught up in those dreams."

"It's understandable." Sidney went through the bag of food they'd picked up, and brought out two cookies. He handed one to Weston. "Well, I don't exactly know the feeling. But I can understand how you might have come to the idea that I was similar to those characters."

"You are, though," Weston insisted. "You're hot, like Sentry. You're passionate about your work, like Saunders. And you care, like Starson did." He noted the bemused expression Sidney wore, and snorted at himself. "Okay, yes, that sounds a little crazy. But you have those qualities."

"Hotness is a quality?"

"It definitely is." Weston reluctantly untangled his hand from Sidney's in order to nibble at his cookie. "And, you know, I did have another dream last night. It was about you, sort of. But it was like that sonnet you like."

In the dream, he'd realized the dream character had flaws, and he loved him still. Granted, that dream had been about marriage; Weston wasn't going to mention that. That might be a bit too soon.

"So, what I'm trying to say is, I'll try not to get caught up in crazy writer's brain," Weston said.

"Okay." Sidney was far too good for him. Most people would be angry at him for being disappointed about not living up to expectations. Sidney just looked calm, understanding, if relieved that Weston had said he would try. "Your dreams do sound fascinating, though."

"They were." Weston grinned to himself as he recalled them. "I wrote down notes on all of them. One day I want to be able to write them down."

Sidney tilted his head, curious. "You haven't been able to?"

"No." Weston shrugged. "I get all nervous." An idea struck him, and he brightened. "Hey, maybe if you're with me when I write, I might not get so nervous. You have this really weird ability to make me not overthink stuff."

"I'm used to flustered artists." Sidney grinned. "But I would like that. We could do dinner again?"

"Or we could just hang out," Weston ventured. "It might be really boring for you, but I like the idea of just hanging out with you."

"I do too." Sidney gave him a fond smile. "How about this weekend? I could bring food over and we could just vegetate on the couch and do nothing."

That sounded absolutely perfect to Weston. "Oh! Henry said he wanted to do lunch with us at some point. Or you. Maybe just you, I don't know. Anyway, I thought sometime this week we could have lunch, you and me, and Henry and Aiko?"

"They want to spend time with me?" Sidney looked surprised at that. "I thought they hated me."

"They did for a while," Weston said sheepishly. "But Henry's a good friend, and once I told him we were dating, I think he realized I have good taste. And Aiko admitted you might not be Satan."

Sidney laughed, grinning widely. "Was that up for debate?"

"It was either Satan or some terrible monster from the deep, like Cthulhu," Weston teased.

"Either way, I'd love to have lunch with them. It would be nice to get to know them, I think."

"Well, I like them, so you might like them too." Weston hoped so, at least. He was also looking forward to meeting more of Sidney's friends—from the stories the man told, he knew some particularly quirky people, which Weston usually found to be a good quality.

"I'm just thankful they no longer think I'm evil incarnate." Sidney huffed in amusement. "I usually get some suspicion due to my job, but it's not normally that extreme."

"We're all a bit strange," Weston apologized, picking up his phone to text Henry. "That's what being in a small business does to you. You go in being just a little weird, because everybody's a bit weird in their own way. And the environment magnifies your weirdness, because it bounces off other people on a regular basis and because we're all too personal with each other. That's my theory."

"There might be some truth to that." Sidney chuckled.

After confirming with Henry that lunch at a later date would be happening, Weston dropped his phone back into his pocket. He took Sidney's hand again, and they sat watching the river and the geese for the rest of their break.

Weston was pretty sure he might be in love. It was something he'd always ridiculed in stories; love so soon was completely unrealistic and didn't happen in real life. But the feeling remained, uncaring if it was unrealistic or not, and instead of freaking out and second-guessing himself, Weston just laid his head on Sidney's shoulder.

He was okay with being unrealistic.


LUNCH with the three of them became dinner hosted at Weston's house, which then became a five-person affair after Henry called to say he was bringing Aiko, and Weston decided shortly after to invite Judy. He wasn't sure why he'd volunteered his lamentable cooking skills for the social gathering—it had been a mere idea when he'd mentioned it to Sidney, an off-the-cuff remark, and Sidney had looked so excited that Weston had just given in.

The hour after work found Weston reluctantly wearing an apron, frantically blowing on his hands. With a sigh, Sidney took him by the wrists, led him over to the sink, and twisted the cold water tap for him.

"And that is why you should remember oven gloves when you try to pull things out of the oven," he reminded Weston, who gave him a baleful glare.

"You were kissing me. And then the thing dinged and I got confused. Hence, forgetting oven gloves."

"Yes, well, I can hardly be blamed for distracting you so thoroughly," Sidney replied slyly. "You don't look badly burned, just a bit of redness."

Weston shook his hands off and carefully dried them, then inspected his fingertips. Sidney was right, thankfully, and the pain was already fading. "This is all your fault in the first place," he told Sidney, turning to inspect the tray Sidney had pulled out—with oven gloves—for him. "This could have just been a nice, easy lunch where all we did was sit around on our asses and get food brought to us."

Sidney laughed lowly, and Weston couldn't be too irritated when he felt Sidney's chest press up against his back, Sidney's arms looping easily around Weston's waist. "I like watching you cook," Sidney murmured, his chin fitting neatly on Weston's shoulder. "You're very haphazard and a little concerning, but the apron's cute."

"The apron is *not* cute," Weston insisted. "It's manly. Extremely manly."

"All right, it's very masculine." Sidney laughed again, pressing a light kiss underneath Weston's ear. "The pie looks good to me."

Sidney was clearly just saying nice things to make Weston feel better; the blueberry pie he'd attempted to make was somewhat lopsided. "I'm sure it'll taste good," Weston sighed. "It had *better* taste good."

"It will," Sidney assured him, tightening his arms around Weston's waist. "And if you think it looks horrible, you can cover it with whipped cream."

Weston brightened. "You are a genius." He made an aborted step toward the fridge. "Unfortunately you're going to have to let me go so I can keep cooking."

"Never." Weston felt the curve of a wicked grin against the side of his neck. "You're just going to have to keep going with me attached to your back."

Because Weston didn't really want to separate from Sidney either, he gamely made a go of it, making Sidney move with him as he fussed around the kitchen. They were laughing by the time Henry and Aiko let themselves in, and Weston only noticed their arrival by Henry's exaggerated groan.

"God, is this what I have to watch for the rest of the night? Dudes cuddling?" But he was smirking as he said it, and a smirk on Henry was a happy smile on anybody else's face.

"You absolutely do," Weston replied. "Get used to it." He gave a belated, "Hi guys, let yourself in and everything."

"Your door was unlocked." Aiko was smiling at them, softer than her usual expression, but it turned tentative when she looked at Sidney. "I'm going to bypass the requisite awkwardness," she announced and stepped over to Sidney to give him a kiss on the cheek.

Sidney obviously didn't receive those very often, because he looked flustered but pleased. "How about we start over?" he offered, putting his hand forward. "Sidney Romero."

Aiko took it in a strong grip that Weston remembered well— she'd nearly crushed his hand the first time he'd met her. "Aiko Sasaki."

Henry took Sidney's hand next. "Henry Ford."

Sidney looked like he was trying not to smile. "Seeing that name on the business records did give me pause, I admit."

"I know." Henry shook his head, amused and exasperated. "You'd think my parents would find a different first name, with that surname."

"I like it," Weston piped up. "And I think you should commit. Stop rebelling by driving Hondas."

He approved of starting over, and he'd say so if he didn't have his hands full trying to make sure he didn't overdo the pasta. Sidney had told him about a trick where he could tell if it was done by cutting it in half to see if there was still white inside, but that seemed far too complicated to Weston. He couldn't even get any out of the pot to check—it kept sliding off the spoon.

While he was distracted by the pasta, he missed the start of conversation happening—Sidney was sympathizing with Henry on the loss of his job, Aiko had found a new target of hatred in Sanderson, and they were chattering away happily as though there'd never been a rift between them at all. Amazed, Weston turned from the cooking pasta to watch them.

Sidney was smiling—somewhat more reserved than his usual with Weston, but Weston felt he could be forgiven that. He didn't know Henry and Aiko well yet, and it was only with trust that Sidney fully opened up.

The doorbell rang, and Judy arrived with a bottle of wine. Weston had invited her earlier that day because although she didn't need to make amends with Sidney, Weston felt she could use some time to destress, and what better way to do so than with food and friends? She had always been quick on the mark—she took one look at Sidney, Henry, and Aiko, and said, "See? I told you Sidney wasn't a force of evil."

"That's still unproven," Weston called from the kitchen. "He *is* making me cook."

"Yes, feeding into my cunning plan to kill you all from improperly prepared food," Sidney said dryly.

"Watch out for the pie, he spat in it earlier," Weston said cheerfully to the tune of following laughter.

Leaving the three to talk, Judy stepped into the kitchen, greeting Weston by handing him the bottle of wine. "I would have brought more, but we all still have to work tomorrow," she apologized.

Weston waved off the apology. "Good thinking. Henry shouldn't be exposed to too much alcohol anyway. He feels compelled to drink it all."

Judy laughed softly, turning to lean back against the counter, keeping Weston company as she watched them. "So. You and Sidney."

"Me and Sidney," Weston echoed, nodding.

"It's working?"

Weston grinned as he stirred the pasta. "It's definitely working."

"I did tell you that you needed to find someone nice and calm." Judy teasingly poked his arm.

"I am *not* that bad," Weston protested.

Judy just laughed at him, and Weston sighed. Okay, maybe he *was* that bad. He wasn't going to tell Judy about his little crisis with fantasy hero expectations; she'd probably just laugh at him more before reminding him he was an idiot.

He pointed her toward the wineglasses, grimacing as he tried to juggle the pasta, the oven gloves, and a wooden spoon. Weston really didn't think he was cut out for this cooking business, but the pasta seemed okay as he drained it, and the sauce he'd been simmering hadn't turned black and molten, so perhaps he was doing okay.

"I'm just glad that Sidney is grounded," Henry announced. He'd wandered into the kitchen too, and was now peering at the sauce. He moved out of the way when Weston batted at him. "Or, he seems grounded. Not like that last guy you dated. What was his name? The himbo."

"I'm going to tell Derek you called him that," Weston tried to threaten, but he was too busy cackling at the thought of Derek's reaction.

Henry snapped his fingers. "That was it. Derek. Sidney's much better for you."

Weston's mocking glee turned into a soft smile as he looked over to see Sidney talking to Aiko. "I'm ridiculously lucky," he agreed. He turned to start pouring the sauce over the pasta and mixing it together. "Now get out of my kitchen. I need space to work so I don't burn everybody with the inevitable spills."

Laughing, Henry and Judy dutifully got out of the way, passing out wine glasses as they went. Weston was pretty sure he performed some kind of godly miracle by *not* splattering sauce everywhere as he served it up, and they crowded around his tiny table to eat.

The pasta was actually surprisingly edible. More than that, it tasted pretty good, so Weston assumed Sidney was just a good influence on him, as well as a good provider of recipes. The wine Judy had brought was rich and mellow, and far from his normal behavior in group situations, Weston was relaxed and chatty, holding Sidney's hand under the table.

By the time they moved on to dessert, Weston felt warm with wine and good company. Sidney seemed to have broken out of his shell and was effortlessly trading teasing quips back and forth with Henry.

Weston was so in love.

"See, you *are* doing the dumb cow eyes." Henry's voice broke him out of his thoughts.

Weston blinked at him. "I am not."

"You are. You're staring at Sidney like he just hung the moon or some shit like that."

Aiko hit Henry on the arm. "Oh, shut up. I think it's cute."

"It is, isn't it?" Sidney smiled slyly. But he squeezed Weston's hand under the table, taking the sting out of the teasing.

The assorted company declared the pie a success too, making Weston feel rather pleased at his effort. If this continued, and he could actually cook with Sidney giving him tips, he might just continue to cook. It was definitely healthier than constantly eating takeout, if nothing else. Cheaper too.

Before it got too late, Henry, Aiko, and Judy bid their farewells. Sidney and Weston were left in the peaceful silence, picking at the last of the pie. The quiet seemed odd in the wake of Aiko's constantly louder-than-normal voice, and Weston found he almost missed it. It had been nice, getting to know her and Judy outside of work.

"I suppose we should clean up," Sidney sighed.

"Uh, no, *you* are not cleaning up. You're a guest." Weston triumphantly stole the last bite of pie.

"But you cooked," Sidney insisted. "It's only fair."

"Only fair that I get to sit on my fat ass and watch you work?" Weston grinned, but he paused then, contemplative. "Actually, that does sound good."

He still beat Sidney in a race to the kitchen, laughing and trying to gently shove Sidney away from the dishes. He almost succeeded, except for when Sidney started drying, seemingly determined to help, and Weston just sighed at him. He couldn't deny, though, that this simple act of washing the dishes with Sidney made him smile to himself, pleased at the domesticity of it all. Weston had never had that with anyone.

At ten, Sidney reluctantly left, and they stood for far too long at the door trading good-bye after good-bye. When Weston finally closed the front door to the tune of Sidney's car rolling out of the driveway, he immediately wanted to invite him back in.

Instead, Weston told himself he would not be clingy and send Sidney a text about how he already missed him, even if it was true.

He would see Sidney at work tomorrow. And later in the week, they had a day together planned. Like how Weston had never achieved domesticity with someone, he'd also never had multiple dates a week, and here he was wanting *more*.

Maybe he'd get a pet to keep him company in the meantime. Something independent that would stare at him dismissively when Weston told it all his problems and how much he missed Sidney. Then again, he couldn't even keep a plant alive, so a pet might not be the best idea.

He'd settle for eagerly anticipating the next date, then.

# Chapter
## Twelve

"I WANT you to read these" was the first thing Weston said to Sidney, shoving papers at him as Sidney stepped through the front door.

The week had gone by excruciatingly slowly, leaving Weston irritated at the new mascot he had to design—a purple parrot—and staring at the clock, silently willing each day to be over faster so the next day would come sooner. The client for the new design, one Mrs. Johnson, had excitedly told him all about Prince's High School mascot, Polly the Purple Parrot, who shouted, "Polly want a victory!" at the opposing team.

Weston had only narrowly avoided violently and repeatedly smashing his head against his desk. Designing things was fun, but the clients were sometimes a little too into their own mascots.

He just prayed they'd never have a repeat of Mr. Gable. Widely known as the man who had gotten rather intimately excited as he ordered a mascot suit, he was still the target of many a joke in their offices, ones that usually left the listener vaguely disgusted.

But Saturday had nonetheless arrived, and Weston had even managed not to flail too much about his clothing choice. All they had planned for the day was hanging out together, so it wasn't as though he needed to get dressed in his best suit. Sidney, damn him, managed to look extremely put together in the most casual of clothes.

"Good morning to you too," Sidney replied, bemused, as he took the papers. "What are these?"

"Those are my notes from the crazy dreams I had," Weston said. "I want you to read them."

Weston had theorized that most people would laugh in his face after such an offer, but Sidney looked touched at the action. "You're okay with me reading these?"

They *were* intensely personal. They told the story of Weston's changing subconscious perception of Sidney, the fear and the paranoia through to the acceptance and the love. But seeing as Weston knew he'd been a giant idiot with his fantasy expectations, it seemed to be a good way of letting Sidney know where he was coming from.

Truth was the most important thing in a relationship. So it was time to bare the most embarrassing parts of himself to Sidney.

"I want you to," Weston said decisively.

Sidney stepped inside, giving him a proper kiss in greeting, which Weston happily returned.

"Hi," Sidney murmured, drawing back, one of his hands lightly curled around the back of Weston's neck. "It's good to see you."

"You too." Weston grinned, leaning in for another kiss. With the door closed, shutting the rest of the world out, Weston took his time with the kiss, languid and content. "The week took too long to go by."

He led Sidney over to the couch and sat down, tugging Sidney down to sit next to him. They wound up nearly on top of each other, Sidney half-turned to face him, a leg hooked over Weston's knee. "Should I read them now?" Sidney asked, getting comfortable.

"I'd say you can read them whenever you want, but since I've spent the morning working myself up into fits about this, yes, I'd like it if you read them now." Weston offered Sidney an embarrassed smile and got a fond laugh in return.

Sidney pressed a kiss to Weston's forehead and settled in to read.

Weston pulled his laptop over to rest it on his legs, then idly clicked through the news of the day. He specifically looked for things that would distract him. He'd poured every thought and feeling about those dreams into his notes, every detail and every piece of characterization. The stories—and, in essence, Weston's subconscious—were right there for Sidney to read.

He supposed that if at any point Sidney were to realize his mistake in dating Weston, this would be it: the moment Sidney realized he was interested in a crazy person.

But there was no immediate leaving, much to Weston's relief. Instead, Sidney occasionally made a thoughtful hum, or an interested one, or gave a quiet chuckle. Weston had to stop himself from obsessively asking what exactly Sidney was reacting to.

Finally, Sidney put the notes down, and Weston tried to look as though he wasn't hanging on every second, waiting for the reaction. "You have an amazing imagination," Sidney murmured.

Weston smiled, feeling slightly flustered. "They're just dreams."

"Weston, do you know what *I* dream about?" Sidney looked bemused. "Turning up to work in my pajamas. Getting stuck in traffic jams. I don't dream up entire worlds and plot lines."

It was better, Weston reminded himself, to gracefully accept a compliment rather than bluster and insist he was nothing special, so he said, "Yeah, I guess they were pretty incredible. I don't normally dream like that."

Sidney shifted on the couch, sitting on the edge so that he could turn to face Weston. "I hope the next words out of your mouth are 'and someday I'm going to write these stories'."

"Hopefully," Weston mumbled, running a hand through his hair. "I did try. I never got anywhere, though."

"You will." Sidney sounded so confident in him, so firm in his belief that Weston could achieve whatever he wanted. "You just need to let go of your nervousness some. A little nervousness, I'm told, can be helpful when creating; it can restrict you from doing anything too over-the-top. But it's too much when you don't write at all."

"It is," Weston agreed with a sigh. "Well, I did say that you have this weird ability to make me not freak out so much about things."

Sidney grinned at him. "Perhaps I'll be your muse."

"I think you already are." Weston leaned forward, putting his arm around Sidney's back. He smiled as he went in for a kiss, the touch of their lips featherlight. "As long as you're not like those Greek muses. They were a bit fickle."

"I am anything but fickle," Sidney promised. They kissed again, languid and easy, even if it was a bit difficult when Weston kept smiling. He was determined, though, sneaking his hand up under Sidney's shirt to feel the warm skin of his back. The action had been intended as casual, but Sidney's reaction to it was anything but—he deepened the kiss, tangling his fingers in Weston's hair to bring him closer.

"You," Weston murmured against Sidney's lips, "are a very good kisser."

Sidney hummed in reply but didn't speak, which was just fine with Weston, because he was more interested in kissing. Words could be left for later. Experimentally, he gently raked his teeth over Sidney's lower lip, and he was rewarded with Sidney's sharp inhale.

"If you keep that up, I'm not going to be able to keep my hands to myself," Sidney said lowly. His eyes were dark, his lips red from their kissing, and Weston didn't think he'd ever seen a more gorgeous sight.

Weston, thus far, had been determined to take this relationship slow. He hadn't had the best luck with dating people so far, and it had seemed like the best option was to change something. So seeing as he usually jumped into bed with his date at the first opportunity, he thought he'd try to avoid doing that with Sidney, to let the nonphysical side of the relationship have time to develop first.

It had seemed like a good idea. But now Sidney was looking at him with want in his eyes, more appealing than any of Weston's dream characters simply because he was *real*.

Fuck going slow.

He twisted, aiming for getting himself into Sidney's lap, and managed to knee him hard in the side of the thigh in the process, drawing a pained yelp from Sidney. "Sorry!" Weston blurted. "Sorry, shit. That went *so* much better in my fantasies."

A wide grin bloomed on Sidney's face as he rubbed at his thigh. "You had fantasies? Did they happen in your dreams?"

"No. I'm not that presumptuous, sadly." Weston frowned apologetically at Sidney and said, tentatively, "I just ruined the mood, didn't I?"

"Not at all." Sidney's hands ran up Weston's sides, then hooked around the back of his neck, neatly pulling him into another kiss. It seemed that Weston had thankfully not ruined the mood at all, because they easily fell back into it. He settled himself more comfortably on Sidney's lap, leaning into him, the force of their kiss pushing Sidney's head back against the couch.

*Definitely* fuck going slow. This was way more fun.

"I didn't bruise you, did I?" he felt the need to ask, concerned, even as he mumbled the words into the kiss. Multitasking was not something that came easily to Weston. "Actually, never mind me. I get told I'm really annoying because I talk too much during sex and worry about everything and—"

Sidney, laughing, shut him up with another kiss. "Shush," he murmured. "Just relax, Weston. We can take this as slow or as fast as you like."

"In that case," Weston replied, "I think we should relocate to my bed. Or any flat surface." Was he being overeager? He didn't know, but at least Sidney wasn't laughing at him, unlike most other people Weston had dated.

"The couch is a flat surface," Sidney said slyly. In a rush of movement, Sidney tumbled Weston onto the cushions with a grin until he had him sprawled on his back on the couch. "You might also want to specify horizontal or vertical."

This position had the pleasant side effect of bringing every part of their bodies into contact, and when Sidney kissed him again, their legs tangled, hips pressing close. "Vertical can be saved for when we're feeling more adventurous," Weston managed, shoving his hands under Sidney's shirt. He painted trails over warm skin with his fingertips, bumping up against the defined curve of Sidney's shoulder blades, tracing down the bumps of his spine.

The shirt clearly needed to go. Weston brought his hands around front, undoing buttons as he caught Sidney in another kiss. It took him longer than he wanted it to, but he eventually managed to shove the shirt halfway down Sidney's arms, then tug it off completely and drop it to the floor. Nudging Sidney, he sat them up again because he wanted to *see* as well as feel.

"Bed?" he asked again, slightly breathless.

"Bed," Sidney agreed.

Weston counted himself lucky he'd decided to make his bed that morning instead of leaving it in the usual mess of blankets. He guided Sidney toward it with a grin, backing him up so that his knees hit the side of the mattress and he fell backward. The sight of him on his bed immediately made Weston want to buy black sheets—he thought Sidney would look amazing against black. As it was, his dusky skin and long limbs looked damn good against white too.

"You are so hot," he said happily, all but pouncing on Sidney. He couldn't get enough of kissing the man, smoothing his hands over Sidney's chest. It wasn't the ridiculously defined torso of fantasy warriors, of Sentry the dragon, but Weston found he didn't care. Sidney was perfect in his own way; he was real, and that made him infinitely better than any dream character Weston could think up.

He wasn't sure when his own shirt came off, but it was discarded along with his jeans, leaving him in boxers that frankly would have been embarrassing if he'd been able to work up the concentration to care. Weston noticed Sidney grinning at the Superman print. "You have a big S on your dick. I like that," he said mischievously, kneeling to mirror Weston's position.

"I'm going to pretend I wore them for you, then," Weston replied, hooking his fingers into Sidney's belt. Arousal ran hot through his blood at just the sight of Sidney shirtless and wanting; he needed to see more skin as soon as possible. But Sidney beat him to the chase, leaning on him until Weston was flat on his back, Sidney's teeth scraping against his collarbone.

The first contact of Sidney's hand on his cock, even through his boxers, made Weston suck in a sharp breath. Sidney didn't waste any time teasing: he kissed Weston hard and rubbed deft fingers over him through the material. Weston couldn't do anything other than groan into the kiss, spreading his legs and pushing up toward Sidney's hand, craving more of the contact.

When Sidney finally slipped his hand beneath Weston's boxers, wrapping properly around his cock, Weston gave his approval by biting at Sidney's lip. He liked Sidney's hands; they were broad and strong, long fingers looking like they belonged on a musician. It turned out that he liked them even better when they were on his cock.

He'd been wanting this for what felt like far too long now to go slow, and Sidney seemed to be on the same page. There was no teasing or idle touches, just a quick yank of his boxers down his hips, and Weston's breath caught as Sidney stroked him with long, firm movements, dragging his palm from base to tip.

"God, you're beautiful," he heard Sidney murmur, and Weston was far too into the current activities to protest or deny it. "And quiet. I think I just found a way to shut you up."

It was probably the most inappropriate thing to do during sex—especially during a first time—but Weston burst into laughter. He looked up to see Sidney grinning down at him. Feeling the need for retaliatory action, Weston rolled them, neatly putting himself on top of Sidney. "Just for that, I'm not playing nice anymore," he warned.

"And how exactly do you not play nice during sex?" Sidney's grin took on a sly shade, and he grabbed Weston's hips. Though Sidney still had pants on, the roll of his clothed cock against Weston's ass made Weston stifle a moan.

Weston actually had no idea, but he was sure he could come up with something. He leaned down, bracing his hands on either side of Sidney's head to kiss him too lightly, teasingly, making Sidney arch his head up if he wanted more contact. "First, I'm guessing the pants have to go," he announced, moving down to start undoing Sidney's zipper. "And then from there, who knows?"

Sidney moved his hips up to help Weston drag his pants and boxers down, and Weston dropped them off the side of the bed. And for a long few seconds, he took the opportunity to marvel at the sight of the man in his bed. Sidney's eyes were half-closed in languid arousal, the line of his limbs relaxed and heavy. Dark hair lay tangled across a white pillow, and as Weston watched, Sidney shifted, spreading his legs to accommodate Weston as he knelt between them.

No wonder Weston had written Sidney into all of his dreams. No wonder his subconscious had made him pop up time and time again. The man was more gorgeous than anybody Weston had ever seen. Forget Sentry and his ripped abs; forget Saunders and his stylish jackets.

With an impish smile, Sidney stretched his arms over his head and wrapped his hands around the bars in the headboard. "I'm waiting on that mean thing you promised," he teased. Sidney looked a shade uncertain, which Weston dispelled by kissing him hard.

"Sorry. I just had to stare," he replied. "You are so ridiculously hot. Why are you even in my bed? I'm way too lucky."

He put his hands on Sidney's shoulders, then trailed his fingers up Sidney's arms, exploring the warm skin and musculature. He discovered Sidney was ticklish in his inner elbows, a fact Weston filed away for later. Taking Sidney's hands from the bars, he curled their fingers together, smiling down at him before moving downward, mapping out Sidney's chest with lips and teeth. He bit gently at the sharp arc of hip bone, grinning to himself at the gasp Sidney made.

He drew farther back, chin rubbing along Sidney's thigh on the way, to get a good look at Sidney's cock—and didn't waste time wrapping his lips around the head and sucking gently. Sidney's moan was music to his ears, and as the man arched his hips up, Weston braced his hands on them, keeping them still.

It had been a while since he'd given a blowjob, but Weston soon remembered exactly how much he enjoyed it. The weight of Sidney's cock on his tongue made his own arousal climb to new heights, so he ducked down, taking more, rubbing his tongue along the sensitive underside. Sidney was talking—saying his name, telling him it felt amazing, cursing here and there—and Weston fought hard not to grin, pleased. It was good to know he hadn't forgotten how to give a good blowjob.

He loved feeling Sidney react underneath him, the subtle tremor in the muscles of his thighs, the way his breathing picked up speed. Weston used his hand on what he couldn't reach with his mouth, tightly gripping the base of Sidney's cock, using his thumb to rub the spot just above his balls. He drew back, playing with the head and grinning when Sidney made little frustrated noises.

"See? Payback," he said smugly.

Sidney was too far gone to give much more than a glare, which wasn't very effective, considering he mostly looked as though he was silently begging Weston to continue. And who was Weston to say no? He eagerly moved back down, sucking Sidney hard and delighting in the loud, ecstatic groan Sidney sounded.

Sidney tangled his fingers in Weston's hair, twisting into the strands around his ear, tugging gently. It was, Weston figured, a message that he was going to come soon, so Weston redoubled his enthusiasm, determined to give Sidney the best damned blowjob ever. Sidney definitely appreciated his efforts, it seemed; when Sidney came, his back arched, muscles tight, a stuttered moan caught in the back of his throat. Sidney collapsed onto the mattress, chest heaving as he drew air in, a flush gathered around his neck and cheeks.

"Is it weird and perverted that I want to take a photo of you right now?" Weston contemplated aloud.

Sidney laughed roughly, the sound of it warm and rolling. "Probably. But I'd be okay with it."

Weston moved up to press a kiss to Sidney's chin and smiled down at him. "As long as I didn't print it and post it around the office. Although I'd be tempted to. It'd be way nicer to look at than all those pictures of cats dangling off branches telling me to hang in there."

With one of Sidney's hands on his arm, he was shifted until they were lying on their sides, facing each other. "Maybe you could draw me," Sidney murmured. "I'd pose for you."

Sidney trailed his hand down Weston's chest, fingertips lightly trailing over Weston's cock. With a hiss, Weston moved into his touch, hitching a leg over Sidney's hips to bring him closer. "I don't think I'd ever be able to draw you well enough," he replied.

Sidney's reply was in the tightening of his grip, the way he started to slowly move his hand over Weston's cock. "I'd still be happy to let you try," Sidney murmured, dark eyes fixed on Weston's face.

Speech began to be more difficult as Sidney sped up the movements of his hand, but Weston gave it a go. "I'll have to practice," he managed, tugging Sidney tight against him. It made the space between them cramped, Sidney having to change the angle of his wrist, but Weston didn't care. It was still good.

He couldn't talk anymore after that. He was too busy feeling the pleasure race through him, muffling his moans against Sidney's lips, bucking into his hand. Weston was even more in love with Sidney's hands then—the way his long, deft fingers twisted around the head of his cock, thumb rubbing gently over the slit with every stroke upward. Minutes dragged and raced by at the same time, and Weston's whole world narrowed down to just them, Sidney's low encouragements and the heat of flushed skin pressed against his.

He came after a particularly hard stroke, digging his fingernails into Sidney's back, uncaring how loud he was being. Sidney seemed determined to draw it out too, dipping down to rub at Weston's balls, making Weston shudder and moan as the last of his orgasm trailed off.

It took a few seconds for Weston to shake off the happy daze, and he relaxed into postorgasm lassitude, grinning and stretching his limbs out. Sidney watched him, a small smile at the edge of his lips as he raked his fingers through Weston's hair, combing it back from his face.

"So. More of that later?" Sidney asked.

"Just what I was thinking," Weston replied, his voice little more than a pleased mumble.

"Weston, it's the middle of the day. You can't go to sleep now." Sidney laughed.

Weston rubbed his head against his pillow, getting comfortable. "Watch me," he mumbled, tightening his grip around Sidney's waist in case he thought he was going anywhere. "Nap with me, Sidney. Midday naps are the best thing ever."

His eyes were closed, and he heard Sidney make an amused little noise as he shifted closer, tugging another pillow over with him. "I haven't taken a nap in years."

"Oh, I'm reintroducing you." Weston found it incredibly sad that Sidney had denied himself the pleasure of naps. "I'm the gold medal champion in napping. I'll take you under my wing and teach you."

He felt Sidney's fingertips trace lightly along his jaw and pass briefly over his lips. "I look forward to it," he heard Sidney say lowly.

Weston gave an agreeing hum, already beginning to drift off with the heavy after-pleasure of good sex. Utterly relaxed, he let sleep claim him.

WAKEFULNESS gently tugged him out of sleep a few hours later, but without the immediate need to get up, Weston let himself hover in that pleasantly hazy in-between space. He slowly opened his eyes.

Sidney was drooling a bit. The sight made Weston grin and bite down on the inside of his cheek so he didn't laugh and wake him. In his sleep, Sidney had rolled onto his back, one arm flung above his head, his lips parted slightly with a quiet rumble of a snore.

Weston was abruptly reminded of the most recent dream he'd had; his gaze went over that one eyebrow that was quirked upward a bit more than the other, the hair that was going everywhere. He was sure Sidney would have bad morning breath and get grumpy when he had to wake up without sufficient reason.

He had flaws. He was perfect.

Weston leaned over and pressed a kiss to Sidney's cheek. Sidney twitched, giving a faint grumble, his eyebrows twisting into a frown as he woke up. Weston was right about the grumpiness, then, and it was adorable.

"How long did we sleep?" Sidney's voice was a mumble, the words tripping over themselves.

"A few hours," Weston replied, watching him fondly. "We don't need to get up right away."

Sidney grunted, apparently happy with that news, and rolled over, shoving his face into Weston's chest. Long minutes passed where Weston smoothed his fingers through Sidney's hair, feeling the movement of his chest as he breathed.

"Tell me the ending," Sidney murmured. "Of those stories that you dreamed."

Surprised, Weston glanced down at him. That was something he hadn't thought about. The dreams had had loose endings, but not solid resolutions.

But as he thought about it, he knew exactly how they would end.

"Well, WingBlade and Sentry teamed up and continued to travel together," Weston said, smiling to himself. He could picture it easily: WingBlade in his rookie amour, Sentry soaring through the blue sky. "They visited as many towns as they could to spread the word that dragons weren't really evil, and they weren't pests, either. They had thoughts and feelings and lives like everybody else. Eventually, the Obsidian Tower started to teach recruits to talk to dragons instead of trying to kill them."

"That sounds nice," Sidney mumbled. He moved, putting his head on the pillow next to Weston's, their noses an inch apart. "What about the detectives?"

"Wickham and Saunders kept solving cases." Weston made an absent arc with his thumb over Sidney's shoulder as he spoke. "They ran into all sorts of crazy and confusing criminals, but they never doubted each other ever again. They got promotions, and Saunders ended up running the joint."

Sidney laughed lowly. "Excellent."

"I think he'd be a good boss," Weston teased, bumping Sidney's knee with his own. "And under his leadership, the officers and detectives solved more crimes than ever and kept criminal activity at an all-time low. Eventually, they grew old together and bought a big house because they couldn't bear to go off and have separate lives after they retired."

"Good. And Wirrex and Starson?"

"Well," Weston said solemnly, "since Cardinal Prime has a stick up its collective ass, they caught Starson, jailed him, and executed all the unregistered people."

Sidney laughed, smacking a hand against Weston's chest. "No, they did not," he insisted. "That's not what happened."

"Oh, isn't it?" Weston grinned, raising an eyebrow. "I thought I was the one who was supposed to be writing these."

"Then by all means, dear author, write away." Sidney kissed Weston, the touch lingering. "But at least give me a happy ending."

Weston smiled softly, adoring, as he looked at Sidney. "Okay. Then how about this: Cardinal Prime did set out to the catch them, but Starson wanted to spend the rest of his life with Wirrex. He delivered the fifty people to his home planet, where they integrated easily. Wirrex made it his life's mission to celebrate the memory of the city Xaridi, so he researched them as much as he could, getting the word out. And he and Starson flew around in their spaceship and had crazy adventures."

"You mean *Starson's* spaceship." Sidney smirked.

"No, after they got into a serious relationship, Starson signed over half of the ownership of the *Nova* to Wirrex," Weston replied loftily. "It's practically marriage in space when you do that."

"Fine, I guess Wirrex can own half the ship." Sidney gave a long-suffering sigh.

Weston chuckled. "I'll be right back." He got out of bed to the sound of Sidney's protesting noise and headed to the living room. After getting his laptop, Weston slipped back into bed, sitting against the headboard and perching the laptop on his legs. "Sorry. Just had a sudden rush of inspiration."

"It's okay." Sidney's smile was fond and easy as he stretched out next to Weston, sitting up. The weight of Sidney's head against his shoulder was a welcome one as Weston opened a new document.

He didn't hesitate as he started typing, his fingers flying over the keys. All of those images, those plot lines and those characters, he could see them so clearly.

Weston knew exactly how to write them. And though he knew he needed to practice writing, to hone his ability, he was *writing*, finally, with no hesitation, no paranoia that it would be horrible, no anxiety about stereotypes now.

He knew the ending to his stories.

ROBIN SAXON, born and bred in New Zealand, lives in the Midwest with partner Alex Kidwell. When not writing or daydreaming about ideas for more stories, Robin is usually found playing MMOs like World of Warcraft, reading, drawing, and fussing over their cats, Starsky and Hutch.

In the rare times when they are not being pestered by their cats, Robin also listens to heavy metal music and enjoys everything from classics like Chaucer to urban fiction, as well as cooking vegetarian meals and inflicting them on Alex.

Find Robin:

- website: http://www.saxonandkidwell.com
- Facebook: http://www.facebook.com/robin.saxon.77
- e-mail: Robin at robin_saxon@yahoo.com.

Also from ROBIN SAXON

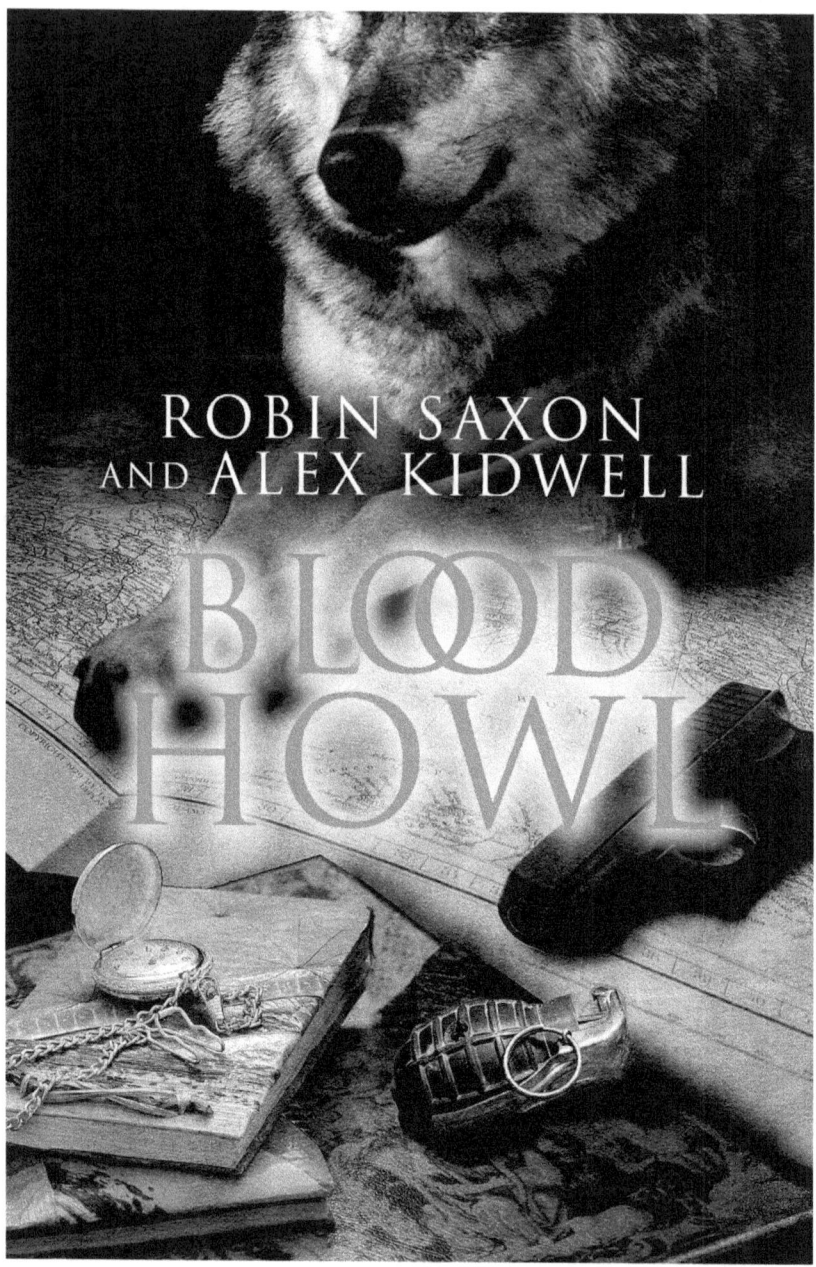

ROBIN SAXON
AND ALEX KIDWELL

BLOOD
HOWL

http://www.dreamspinnerpress.com

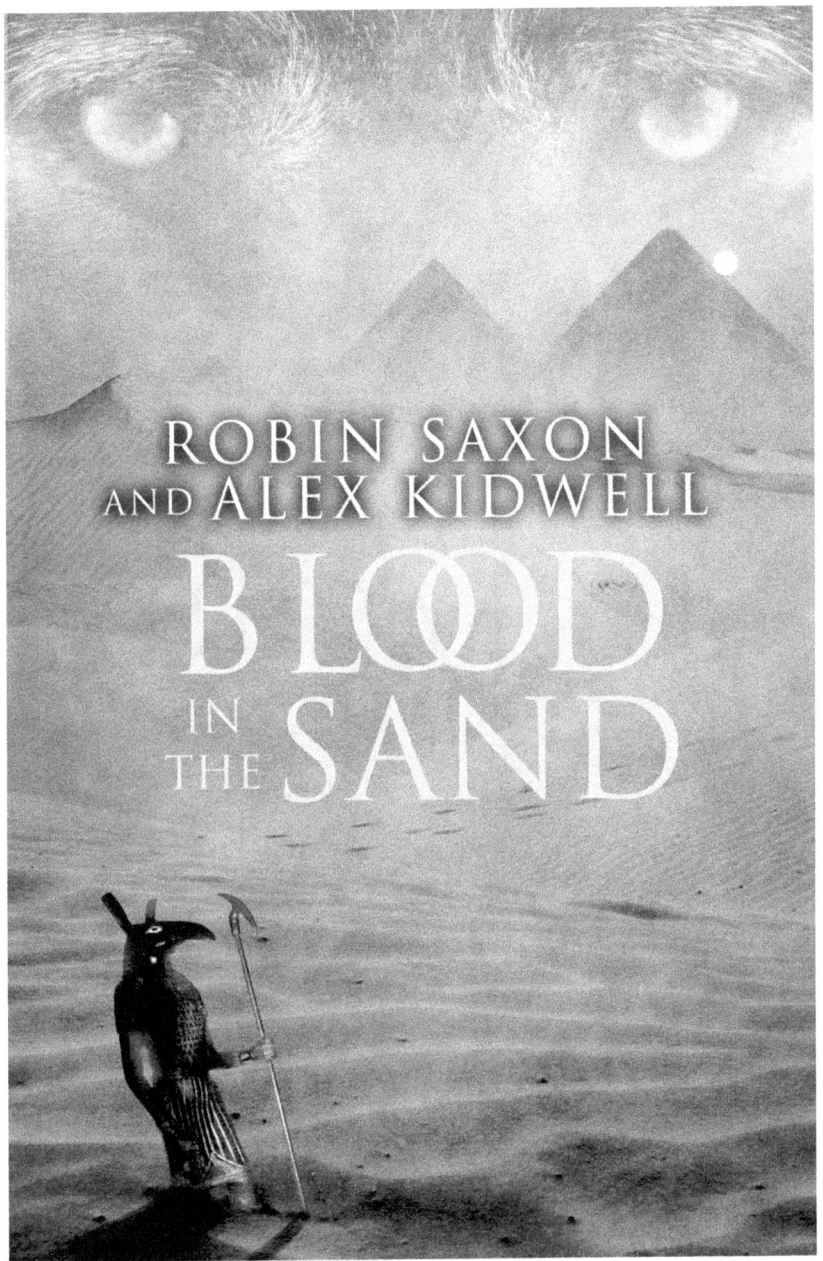

ROBIN SAXON
AND ALEX KIDWELL

BLOOD
IN THE SAND

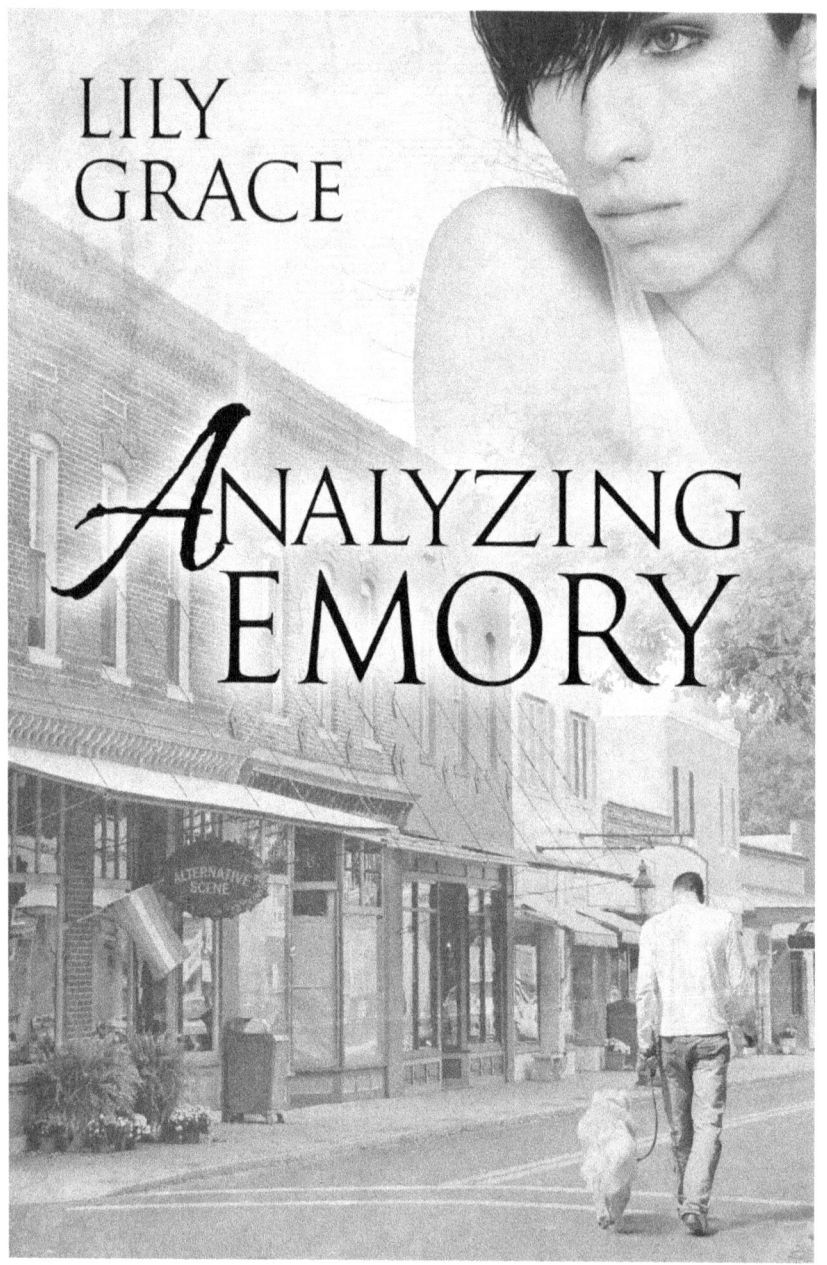

BROWN-EYED
DEVIL

EVAN GILBERT

www.ingramcontent.com/pod-product-compliance
Lightning Source LLC
Chambersburg PA
CBHW060103260626
47160CB00005B/1774